THE FLOW I: PLIMOTH PLANTATION
(THE PREQUEL)

WENDY ROSE WILLIAMS

6/17/19

Dear Karen -

Thank you for being such an incredible friend all these years!

Love,
Wendy

THE FLOW I: PLIMOTH PLANTATION (A PREQUEL)
COPYRIGHT 2018 WENDY ROSE WILLIAMS

BOOK CATEGORY: FICTION/ GHOST

FIRST EDITION (MAY 2019)
FIRST PRINTING (MAY 2019)

ISBN-13: 978-1546528258
ISNG-10: 1546528253

PUBLISHED VIA CREATESPACE INDEPENDENT PUBLISHING
NORTH CHARLESTOWN, SOUTH CAROLINA

COVER DESIGN AND FORMATTING BY LEILANI DOORNBOSCH
WEBSITE: CUSTOMCOVERPRO.COM

THE FLOW SERIES

'We're all just walking each other home.'
--Ram Dass

PRAISE FOR THE FLOW I: PLIMOTH PLANTATION (THE PREQUEL)

"The writing in this book is entertaining and filled with humor and ease. It is great story-telling and easy to read."
- *Jennifer Green*
  (Los Angeles, California)

'I have literally known the soul called Wendy Rose Williams for thousands of lifetimes. In this lifetime, she has been an invaluable Past-Life Regression Expert who has helped me heal from traumatic past lives. As a practitioner she has impeccability, integrity, an outstanding business practice with her confidentiality code of honor and professional ethics. If you need a past life regression I highly recommend Wendy's services.'
- *Robin Alexis, host 'Mystic Radio'*
  (Mt. Shasta, California)

'The author intertwines present day with a past life story that is vivid, interesting and plausible. The characters are real people and the reader clearly gains an understanding into the positive use of past-life regression to heal both the present and past. I look forward to the next book.'
- *Ellen Kaspi*
  (Seattle, Washington)

'I found this book to be very enjoyable and well-edited – I notice spelling and punctuation. The back jacket was a good explanation of the story. I loved the author's note – so multidimensional. The story flows well and it is fascinating! I am interested in the characters, especially Ann Warren Little and Gwendolyn Rose. What a wonderful gift to humanity this book is. Hooray for you for writing these books. Living something is one thing and writing about it is another thing entirely – lots of work. I will follow your career with interest.'

- *Thia Rose, RN, CCHT, QHHT Practitioner*
  (Colorado)

'This is a wonderful book that can be classified in several categories, encompassing all the following: a love story, spiritualism, reincarnation, autobiography, history, and historical fiction. If historians read this book, will they use it as fact or fiction, since it is factual per the Akashic Record?'

- *Dr. Michael Tran*
  (Manhattan, Kansas)

CONTENTS

DEDICATION

This book is dedicated to the numerous family members and friends who incarnated with me in the 1600s at Plimoth Plantation, and again in my present life.

A tip of the hat to Captain William Pierce for bringing the Richard Warren family safely to America in the years 1620 and 1623; to my loving parents Elizabeth and Richard Warren; to my birth mother; to my neighbor and best friend Abby; to my older sister Mary; to my little brother Nathaniel; to the wonderful man who was King Philip; and to my devoted cat Midnight as well as to my former husband.

Blessings for the many healers who helped me with serious energetic challenges experienced during my rapid spiritual awakening, including how to best heal my past life as Ann Warren Little of Plimoth Plantation.

My deepest gratitude to the profoundly gifted Mystic Robin Alexis. Robin helped me rebirth myself in countless ways during the years 2013 to 2017. I am forever grateful.

Blessings for Amy, Larry, Lisa, Darcy, Rus, Laurie, Anh, Donya, Ben, and Irina. I appreciate your empathy and assistance with my healing and releasing of the Plimoth lifetime more than words can express. Thank you to Veteran Jon Nordin for helping me decipher military spending.

My sincere gratitude to my mother Elizabeth Elliott for many hours spent editing my endless split infinitives; creative yet totally incorrect roman numerals for the original chapter headings; and for her repeated careful proofreading.

My warmest thanks to the generous beta readers including Becky Buchko, Laurie Regan, Karen Peck, Rich Vernadeau, Rus Sullivan, Bruce Bradley, Christine Luque,

Amy Mowry, Susan Edelman, Ellen Kaspi, Michael Tran, Jennifer Green and Thia Rose.

Your thoughtful comments, questions and recommendations improved the readability of this novel. Any factual errors are mine and mine alone.

AUTHOR'S NOTE

This metaphysical fiction account was inspired by events in my life. In August of 2010 I met the soul mate I contracted with to wake me up spiritually. I didn't fully comprehend what was happening for several years, though I sensed keenly life would never be the same.

Our meeting felt not only pre-destined, but a unique opportunity for me to enrich my life *if* I had the courage to jump off the proverbial cliff into uncharted waters.

'Simon' *(name changed to provide confidentiality)* introduced me to Dr. Michael Newton's best-selling 'Journey of Souls.' Dr. Newton's carefully documented findings from more than 7,000 hypnotherapy clients during his forty-year career resonated deeply for me.

I had my first Past-Life Regression in November of 2011 with a superb Newton hypnotherapist. A year later I returned for a four-hour 'Life-Between-Lives' spiritual regression to my pure soul state, i.e. when not incarnated in a body.

I resolved my challenges with anxiety during my first Past-Life Regression. It was so gratifying to release a lifetime of anxiety during a single two-hour session! That's how powerful therapeutic hypnotherapy can be with healing and releasing energy that no longer serves us.

I began waking up hard and fast, yet without any conscious knowledge of how to appropriately manage my energy, including how to be sovereign in my own field.

I experienced tremendous fear when I realized I was attracting low vibration energy that wasn't mine. I wished fervently at times there was a way to slam the lid shut on the Pandora's Box of my spiritual awakening, but the train had already roared out of the station.

I struggled to first accept and then address my own energetic issues. Shortly after my incredible Life-Between-Lives session, my world tipped upside down during a pivotal phone call with my long-time friend Abby.

A female ghost visited Abby's home, and had not wanted to leave. Abby had to work hard to remove the heartbroken ghost and wasn't confident she had gone to the Light.

The possibility of ghosts even existing stretched my belief system hard. But I knew I had experienced what I could only describe as a ghost or apparition over a four-year period several decades earlier when I was a newlywed.

But what rocked my world view so hard more than twenty years later as I spoke with Abby was the realization that the heartbroken ghost appeared to be ME from an earlier life!

This was a tremendous and unwelcome shock. I didn't know this could even happen.

I began to investigate as methodically as I could what was occurring. I immediately saw this disincarnated (not in a body), Earth-bound energy couldn't stay. She was causing serious disruptions to my current life and now negatively impacting friends, including Abby.

I had to take responsibility, though I hadn't a clue how to help this young female ghost. I only knew I had to 'get it together' – quite literally.

The ghost and I needed to make peace. I very much needed a soul retrieval of that lifetime.

But who was this broken-hearted ghost? How could we BOTH be here at the same time? Why hadn't she – I – gone Home when she dropped her body?

My incredible journey to find, validate, learn from, heal and release, be thankful for, amazed by, and eventually celebrate so many of my past lives ratcheted up hard when Abby informed me I had a ghost in early 2013.

**

I had no intent to write a book. I wasn't a writer, though I was an avid reader and earned a bachelor's degree in English before my master's degree in Business Administration.

I had never heard of the genre I was being repeatedly guided to write. What was 'metaphysical fiction?'

I googled it – yes, metaphysical fiction was a small niche category that included 'The Alchemist,' 'The Celestine Prophecy', and 'Jonathan Livingston Seagull.'

But I had no *time* for this huge project, especially once my planned novella quickly snowballed into a novel, which became a trilogy, and then required this prequel.

Nor did I feel I had the writing or editing skills, the design and layout knowledge, the patience, the self-discipline, the financing, or the publishing and book promotion expertise or connections required.

Yet it was becoming increasingly clear my life purpose included helping others to wake up spiritually, to balance their energy and ego, and to get their feet firmly on the ground.

My Spirit Guides repeatedly asked me to do this soul mission work by writing, teaching and mentoring others on the path, including being interviewed live about reincarnation, past lives and my metaphysical experiences.

Yikes! Didn't my Guides understand I had a *profound* fear of public speaking? I didn't know at the time that I, like many people, had been persecuted, tortured and killed for speaking my truth.

Doesn't make one fond of public speaking.

This may be why public speaking is the greatest fear in our culture – more so than death. My subconscious carried the memories and the crippling fear at the soul level as emotions are timeless.

I didn't have a clue how to heal and release this fear – this energy that didn't serve me. Fortunately, my primarily positive scribe, writer, storyteller, oracle, counselor, hypnotherapist and teacher past lives began to bubble to the surface, balancing the scales.

Turns out I'd done a lot of writing and public speaking and lived to tell the tale.

I discovered that my Civil War diary was published. A diary – that was easy. Anyone can write a diary. Was I making this too hard? I sensed multiple Guides nodding yes.

I quickly ordered a copy of 'A Woman's War Time Journal' by Dolly Sumner Lunt Burge. Holding that slim little book in my hands proved I could be a published author.

I felt I'd been a writer before when I was Dolly, during Sherman's March to the Sea, designed to break the spirit of the South during the Civil War.

I learned my experiences as Oregon Wagon Train leader Jesse Applegate were published in a weekly newspaper column. Newspaper column – hmmm, this wasn't rocket science.

Was I allowing a self-limiting belief that 'I'm not a writer' to stop me from fulfilling my life purpose and larger soul mission? Again, I sensed multiple Guides nodding 'yes.'

I thoroughly enjoyed finding my life as an obscure, married female writer. I learned over time we'd lived in tiny Othello, Oregon Territory (now Washington State) in the 1800s.

I had the good fortune to make a past life pilgrimage to Othello with Simon, who helped me wake up spiritually in my current life. I believe Simon was my husband in that life. I feel we even found the farm we lived on, as it was next to the cemetery we visited to search for our own graves.

I learned I may have had a past life as Anne Hathaway, Will Shakespeare's wife. I blocked that possibility for a time as questioned whether it was an ego trick as Shakespeare is so well-known. It could be fantasy or delusion, or simply a mistake on my part.

Was I attention-seeking? No. Did I want to be famous? Heck no! I thrive on peace and tranquility. Could I simply be wrong about any of these past life identifications? Absolutely!

I struggled to accept I may be one of the Louisa May Alcotts, though I don't feel I wrote 'Little Women,' Louisa's most beloved and well-known work. I believe I wrote the lesser-known 'Hospital Sketches' about my experiences as a volunteer nurse for the Union Army during the Civil War, as well as 'Rose in Bloom' simply because it was marketable. (I feel I had a major role in supporting my parents and sisters as Louisa May.)

My belief is multiple souls can take their turn in the same lesson-rich lives. What if our incarnations are like play runs, cast with different characters, at different times?

Hence there could be multiple Louisa May Alcotts, just as there could be multiple William Shakespeares as time is continuous, and better represented by a loop than a line.

I feel in my heart I wrote a beautiful 'Book of Love' as Mary Magdalen – another past life I blocked for almost a year.

The mere possibility that I was one of many Mary Magdalens initially gave me what author and film director Rich Martini calls 'Catholic brain freeze.'

I'm not Catholic, but we all understand the FIGHT-FLIGHT-FREEZE limbic response that occurs when we experience abject fear.

These are examples of how one's ego and energy need to be strong and balanced to address portions of one's own past life energy and lessons, particularly when Biblical, historical or famous past lives present.

***

It's so freeing to release the self-imposed fear of 'What will other people think?' This has been one of my most challenging life lessons.

Wayne Dyer said, 'What other people think of me is none of my business.' I repeat that often to help me master my life lesson of self-acceptance.

My writer energy was building via these past life memories returning. I was incredibly fortunate my first short story, 'A Tiny Bow and Arrow' won a writing contest and was published in 'The Best of Spiritual Writers Network 2014: An Inspirational Collection of Short Stories and Poems.'

My writer energetic blueprint was created with the publication of those five simple pages. *'A Tiny Bow and Arrow'* is the story of my first conscious experience with a portal opening. It's also encouragement to love again.

I didn't write the following story in the traditional sense. I more simply heard it as Ann Warren Little narrated her life story for me.

I finally understood why she didn't go Home for so long after living at Plimoth Plantation during the years 1623 to 1676. Over time I fully grasped not only the source of her heartbreak, but how to heal it, and in doing so, heal myself.

Healing and releasing pain and other energy that no longer serves us changes everything! It allows us to fully be at peace and to experience love and joy.

***

Plymouth, Massachusetts is now spelled with a 'y' but the letter 'i' was used in the 1600s to distinguish it from Plymouth, England. I chose to use the 1600s spelling as it feels most authentic to Ann's life and times.

Most of this story takes place in the 17th century. When the timeline moves to present day or into time periods other than Ann's lifetime, italics are used as a visual cue to help denote we're jumping timelines.

-*Wendy Rose Williams (September 2018)*

Chapter 1

My name was Anna Warren when I incarnated in the 1600s. I was always simply called Ann. I spent most of my life as an early settler, or 'First Comer' at Plimoth Plantation, also called 'The New Colony.' This land later became part of the Commonwealth of Massachusetts in the United States of America.

I was the second oldest of five daughters. Our father Richard was a successful London grower and merchant. Our mother lived just long enough to birth five daughters like clockwork every two years between the years 1610-1618.

Sadly, my memories of Mother quickly faded. I was only six when she went Home. I would occasionally tell my three younger sisters charming stories about Mother upon request as it made them happy.

I was not clear myself as the years rolled by if my stories were fact, or fiction. If you tell a story the same way long enough it takes on a life – a sustainable energy – of its own.

***

Richard Warren was born April twelfth, 1585 in Shoreditch, Middlesex England. Father married Elizabeth Walker as his second wife on April 14th, 1619 in Great Amwell in Hertfordshire England.

Elizabeth's father's name was Augustine. I don't recall her mother's name as it's been over three hundred years.

Elizabeth Warren's soul incarnated as my mother Elizabeth in present time, as my mother and stepmother at Plimoth switched roles in my current life.

***

Elizabeth became an incredible mother to us over time. Once I was an adult – especially once I became a mother myself – I came to ever more admire and appreciate her immense sacrifice and kindness in not only taking care of another woman's five daughters as her own, but for truly loving, guiding, protecting and providing for us during her remarkably long life of ninety plus years. She seemed to love us as completely as the two sons she would later bear my father at Plimoth.

We appreciated her for so many reasons, including Elizabeth's incredible strength, intelligence, wisdom, and even temperament. Elizabeth Walker Warren stood out in a time when women blended in and were most often only a reflection of their husbands and children.

***

Why did we choose to abandon our comfortable life in England for such an uncertain future in the New World? In 1619 a law was passed in England making it illegal to discuss religion even in private homes. This was enough oppression from the Crown that many chose to leave in search of religious freedom. Others became Pilgrims – meaning travelers – to seek improved financial fortunes.

I remember waving my hand more and more sadly from the docks when my father finally successfully departed. I was nine years old when Father left for the New World aboard the Mayflower in 1620.

We were still gesturing with all our might when his ship had sailed out of sight. Perhaps we were afraid to stop waving as then he would truly be gone.

It was the Mayflower's third attempt to sail for America. The first was in July of 1620. Imagine going through the heart-wrenching emotions of saying goodbye and enduring that difficult parting not once, not twice, but three times!

We all wondered when we would see Father again. We couldn't bear to think *if* we would see him again.

***

As I thought back to my father's departure aboard the Mayflower on September 6th, 1620, Elizabeth had done a brilliant job comforting five extremely somber girls aged three to eleven.

She distracted us with stories about what mischief the two dogs on board the Mayflower would get into. We could see a huge English Bull Mastiff and a small Springer Spaniel running about on board that day, barking excitedly.

We learned dogs are often taken aboard long voyages to protect the food rations from rats. I was quite frightened at the thought of rats as I had heard they could be vicious and were thought to carry disease.

A Bull Mastiff is a large and powerful dog that weighs as much as 110 to 130 pounds. They were originally bred to guard estates and are fiercely protective.

We didn't realize at the time that the large Mastiff bitch was also being brought for protection in the New World along with the guns and cannons. Those we could not miss seeing being loaded aboard the Mayflower. I understood guns were used in hunting, but cannons? What sort of place was this New World?

No one was willing to state aloud would Father be safe. And would we be able to prosper alone in England without him?

What would happen when we went to join him in the New World? What would our lives really be like? Despite my young age, I knew there would be no turning back – this was a decision for a lifetime.

I heard adults describe the hundred-foot long Mayflower as a 'typical merchant vessel of our day.' I wasn't sure what that meant.

I counted that she had at least six sails that I heard were adjustable – sailors either 'put on' or 'took off' sail depending how much wind there was and how rough or smooth the seas were.

The grown-ups, especially the men, talked about the Mayflower's square-riggings, beaked bow, and high castle-like superstructures both front and back, which were called fore and aft.

I heard those areas were to protect the cargo and crew in the worst weather. But what about the passengers – where would Father be?

The seamen boasted that the Mayflower's boxy shape and deep drag made her highly stable but admitted beating against the wind could be painfully slow at times. A journey of three thousand miles would thereby take several months as Father's ship wouldn't skim lightly over the seas.

It would be a long time before we could hope for a letter from him confirming he was safe in the New World.

***

The Mayflower passengers were slated to travel to a small settlement called Jamestowne. There they would join a small number of our fellow Englishmen.

Jamestowne – later spelled as Jamestown without the final 'e' – would become part of the state of Virginia.

We prayed for Father's safety and good health daily, both as a family and on our own. Prayer was part of the fabric of our lives. It provided comfort and clarity of thought and was a way to express our gratitude to God.

Christopher Jones was the Ship's Master for Father's voyage. He was part owner of the Mayflower ship. Captain Jones was a highly-experienced Ship's Master of approximately fifty years of age when he ferried Father and the other passengers to the New World.

Ship's Masters later became known as Sea Captains. In our day the term Sea Captain was reserved specifically for the militia, but the word usage later broadened.

The Mayflower was rated at one hundred and eighty tons, which meant her hold would accommodate one hundred and eighty casks of wine. But what did that equate to in people?

We could see what looked like at least a hundred or more people attempting to board the ship with Father. Would they all fit? How would they get along in such close quarters for months on end?

The Mayflower was classified as a 'sweet ship' since the seamen remarked some of the wine inevitably spilled. They joked raucously the sweet aroma of the wine would help temper the stench of the bilge.

I hadn't a clue what 'bilge' was.

I would learn three years later during my own perilous voyage aboard the Anne of London that bilge smells disgusting! It becomes increasingly vile the longer you are at sea. It was a horrific and pervasive smell you couldn't escape except for a few precious moments topside.

But we were down below deck in the cargo hold for most of the grueling journey, as were the Mayflower passengers. Be clear the Mayflower class of ships were cargo ships. They were not built for passenger comfort.

My Future Self Gwen spit out her tea in surprised laughter when she saw National Geographic's 'Saints and Strangers' depict the Mayflower passenger deck. It showed comfortable-looking beds with curtains for privacy for each family, lamps to provide lighting, and a much higher ceiling than we endured in the 'tween deck cargo hold area.

***

The core group of Mayflower passengers was members of a reformed Christian church. They had originally emigrated from England to Leiden, Holland to worship freely. In separating from the Church of England they committed treason and faced prison – or worse – if caught. It was extremely dangerous to go against the Crown.

These English citizens later became known as 'Separatists,' or 'Saints,' but we didn't use those terms. They were derogatory and risky in our day.

***

In my current incarnation as Gwen I didn't consciously know the term Separatist was used to describe some of the Plantation families. Yet this was the word I used to best describe my family's politics and/ or religion during my first Quantum Healing Hypnotherapy session in 2013 when the hypnotherapist specifically asked me – asked Ann, who was speaking through me at the time – this question.

This lent a lot of credence to my detailed memories shared during my session. I amazingly spoke quietly and confidently as Ann Warren Little for over an hour, as did my use of the term 'daub and wattle construction' to describe how our homes were built.

I didn't recall that construction technique until I had the memory aid of a Quantum Healing Hypnotherapy session. I didn't remember it consciously in my current life, though it's certainly possible I had known it at one time and forgotten it.

Cryptomnesia is the term for when a forgotten memory returns without being recognized as such and is believed to be new and original information. Cryptomnesia is the bane of reincarnation researchers.

Many researchers focus on finding young children who appear to recall a past life. The researcher then painstakingly investigates the most promising cases with the assumption there has not been outside influence or decades of forgotten information that may exist with an adult subject.

***

In the 1600s we Pilgrims referred to ourselves as 'Planters,' referring to the Plimoth settlers who farmed, or 'Adventurers,' referring to the men and a few women who financed the original colony.

Many of us were from the Nottinghamshire region of England, home to the fabled Robin Hood. Most Colonists came from the east and south of England with the majority from London.

The colony's investors included John Pierce, another Mayflower owner along with Captain Jones. The patent granted to John Pierce and Associates in the years 1619 to 1620 determined the course of my life in profound ways.

John Pierce recruited about fifty individuals from the London area to join the group from Leiden, Holland. This is how Father became an original settler at Plimoth Planation in 1620, and how the Warren Family became part of 'The Great Migration.'

Becoming part of this key migration led to my reunion in 1623 with my primary soul mate.

We met again in 2010 to allow us to close out old energy that no longer served us, including from Plimoth Plantation.

John Pierce selected his brother William as one of the principal Ship's Masters for the Mayflower ships. Multiple dangerous long voyages were planned between England and the New World. Expert mariners were vital.

Father was recruited to what would become 'New Plimoth' because he was a successful grower and merchant in England. These skills would be critical as we would have to provide our own food, water, shelter, warmth, protection, and more.

Our currency would be essentially useless. There would be little to buy, although we hoped we would still be able to trade for or purchase some clothing, footwear and other necessities from England and other parts of Europe.

We had no idea if we would be able to trade with any Native people. Would any Natives be friendly, or were we risking our lives? Would there even be any other people?

Was the land truly unpopulated as we were told by our King when he originally claimed the land and sent us to colonize it?

***

We were so proud of Father and the other original Colonists for their bravery. Many Colonists sought religious freedom and some a more prosperous or otherwise fulfilling new life.

A few were frankly adventurers, according to the adult whisperings. I also heard 'All were needed' to settle the New World.

An incredible twenty thousand of us emigrated during the Colonial America era over the next fifty years. We reproduced at a prolific rate, including the Warren family.

***

I return to my narration of Father's departure now that I have provided some background to my story. The Mayflower passengers did not have an easy start to such a dangerous, life-changing passage.

On August 5th, 1620, the Speedwell and the Mayflower set sail for northern parts of Virginia. By August 13th, eight days later, many were angrily calling the Speedwell 'the Leak Well.'

The two ships put into Dartmouth. The Speedwell was repaired, and the two ships set sail again on August 23rd. Both ships had to put back into Plymouth (England) as the Speedwell still was not seaworthy.

***

Captain William Pierce shared his belief with me years later that the Speedwell was over-masted when she was re-outfitted, meaning too large a mast was placed on her. An over-masted ship will later unexpectedly leak along her seams. There is too much drag when water pounds with great force on the bottom of a ship once she's under hard sail.

William told me many things during our time at Plimoth. I believed every word that fell from his lips. I was young and naïve. And I loved him with all my being.

Some of what he told me – or carefully omitted speaking of – did not serve me well. Discernment is a crucial skill, as well as one I clearly lacked.

But it takes two to tango. It took me hundreds of years to own my part in what happened to my soul after my death.

But I'm getting ahead of my story...

***

I return to Father's departure. The Mayflower finally sailed alone for the New World with Father aboard, her destination the fledgling Virginia Colony.

Some passengers had to be left behind in Plymouth, England. Otherwise they would arrive too late in the season to build shelter and to find enough food if the trip was delayed again.

Despite our fine relationship with our stepmother, we girls so longed to reunite with Father! It wasn't until I was married myself that I could begin to appreciate what it must have really been like for Elizabeth alone in London without her husband. She was essentially a newlywed, and a woman caring by herself for her husband's five daughters when she had not yet had children of her own.

Elizabeth was everything to us during those three years in London. It foreshadowed our future more than we knew.

***

We lived for Father's letters during the lengthy time we remained behind in our large, comfortable home in England. But his letters were few and far between.

Much of the news we received was extremely sobering. Elizabeth especially must have mourned friends who perished at the Colony during the first few years. Most died from scurvy, pneumonia, influenza, exposure and starvation.

Our stepmother must have been extremely worried about her husband. Yet she managed to shelter us from this and to allow us our childhood until about age eight. We were then expected to begin to contribute to the family and later to society at large.

Father's letters briefly narrated the many hardships during the Mayflower's challenging passage. We learned much more once we joined him in Plimoth as he read aloud to us from his diary.

There were also moments of great joy and celebration during the Mayflower's long sailing. A baby was born to the Hopkins during the trip and appropriately named Oceanus.

A second baby was born aboard the ship in the harbor before everyone began living on-shore at Plimoth after the first few homes were painstakingly built. The Whites named him Peregrine, meaning 'Wanderer.'

***

Father wrote to us that on November 9th, 1620, the crew and passengers of the Mayflower were overjoyed to spot the tip of Cape Cod, named for its plentiful cod fishing. But they were far north of the Jamestowne destination authorized in John Pierce's patent. They attempted to sail south to Virginia but were defeated by treacherous shoals.

Shoals are sand or gravel banks which can strand your ship, seriously damage it, or even tear out the bottom. They are a serious risk to any ship, particularly one with a deep drag like the Mayflower merchant ship construction.

Much of this class of ships rode under the water line, like an iceberg. She didn't skim the surface lightly.

Merchant ships rode low both for stability and for storage purposes. They were certainly *not* designed for passenger comfort.

Chapter 2

Father would later tell us how on November 11th, 1620, the Mayflower anchored off Provincetown, located on the northern tip of the curving, distinctive Cape Cod. This land mass would later become part of the state of Massachusetts, named for the native tribe.

The Mayflower Compact was drawn up and signed by almost all the men aboard. Its purpose was to establish a provisional governmental structure until a new patent could be obtained from those funding the New Colony. The original patent was to settle in northern Virginia, so the Mayflower Compact was now needed as an interim proclamation.

I find it amazing that over time the Mayflower Compact became ranked with the Declaration of Independence and the United States Constitution as a seminal American text.

Father explained to us how almost every man aboard either signed his name or marked the Compact with the letter 'X' if he was illiterate. Some men were too ill to sign, and a few seamen who had signed on for only one year were not asked to make their mark.

He told us how all the men crowded into the Great Cabin – which measured about thirteen by seventeen feet – to hammer out the agreement and to then sign it. John Carver was chosen as the first Governor for a planned period of one year.

Not a single woman helped plan or sign the Mayflower Compact, not that many were aboard the maiden voyage. This reflected our times as women were not treated equally.

***

Gwen saw the original Mayflower Compact on a 2013 episode of 'Who Do You Think You Are' with Ashley Judd.

She held her breath as this precious text was opened by a careful gloved hand to show the well-known actress the original signatories.

Gwen immediately burst into unexpected tears when she saw Richard Warren's signature on her television screen. This is a classic indicator of a past life, as emotions can remain strong at the soul level.

I feel I have the same father again this lifetime. I believe he was also the 1800s well-known transcendentalist Amos Bronson Alcott who lived in Concord, Massachusetts. Amos was Louisa May Alcott's father.

***

We return to Richard Warren's narration. Father told us that after the men crafted and signed the Mayflower Compact, a party was sent to explore for the most suitable settlement site. The men were led by Plimoth's military leader Captain Myles Standish.

Things were becoming desperate aboard the Mayflower at that time. Captain Jones referred to her as a hospital ship.

Ship's Master Jones was unable to discharge his passengers and return to England as too many of his crew had died or were gravely ill. That was fortunate for the passengers in some ways as no shelter had yet been built.

On December 8th, 1620, the Native people – called the Wampanoag – were encountered for the first time while the scouting team explored where to best settle.

This became known as 'The First Encounter.' Shots and arrows were exchanged with the first shot fired by Captain Standish. Amazingly no one was injured or killed.

Father said we Colonists quickly learned a sobering truth. An Indian can fire off more deadly arrows much more quickly than we could discharge our rifles and flintlocks. They didn't work reliably in the wet weather and required lighting.

It was the wrong time of year to begin to build shelter and to try to plant crops, due in part to the departure delays from July to September. In hindsight, we should have sailed in late winter to early spring.

We English had seriously underestimated how much colder it would be in New England than in England, and what it would be like to try to build enough shelter and to find adequate food in full winter in an unknown area, with so many seriously ill, dead or dying.

We had planned for the more temperate Virginia. Father told us solemnly that some of the men endured frostbite so severe during the early exploring that their precious boots and shoes had to be cut off their feet.

He told us with chagrin the exploring parties had made other serious mistakes before the First Encounter. Our men stole some of the Native corn buried graveside for the departed, and likely took treasured personal effects from inside their tent-homes.

We later learned the Wampanoags called their homes wigwams. Some tribes call them tee-pees, which is spelled tipis.

I can't imagine how cold and frightened our men must have been to have behaved in this deplorable manner. Over time we came to appreciate the Indian tribes' bitter history with voyagers arriving by ship.

Explorers had killed and injured some of their people and had carted some off to be sold into slavery. I have past life memories of an earlier life as a Wampanoag male captured, sold and transported by ship to a foreign land.

This was the volatile reality at the New Colony from its inception. Captain Standish would add to the powder keg, eventually resulting in war.

Standish and I would not be friends. I found him to be quite the *arsworm!* I am confident you will be able to translate that pejorative to its modern-day equivalent.

***

I encountered Myles Standish's soul in a future incarnation in the early 2000s as my Future Self Gwendolyn. He was an unscrupulous business competitor.

Gwen first met 'Standish' at her place of employment when she discovered him copying down her company's proprietary customer list. She challenged him regarding his actions. He lied and told her he was preparing for a meeting with the manager of her department.

Gwen quickly confirmed he did not have a meeting with her direct supervisor. She gave him the choice of leaving immediately and not returning to her department, or that she would call Security. He sauntered out the door a bit slowly, acting as if it was his plan all along.

Within 30 minutes Gwen found a current photo of him on-line and circulated it throughout her entire department as a persona non grata. She put in a written request Security ban him from the campus, steam coming out of both her ears.

When her request was denied a few weeks later as a potential restraint of trade, she worked with top management to convert their department to a locked unit.

Unfortunately, the fox was fully in the hen house and the former Standish first picked off two of her largest clients. She immediately went to her customers in-person to shore up client relations at the highest level.

Gwen felt some of the old Myles Standish energy present the first time she saw him in-person. Here was a direct competitor brazenly copying down her hard-earned customer list posted on the wall in Customer Service as part of their department's courier route.

She wasn't spiritually awake enough to hear 'Past life energy!' from Spirit as she often does now. Gwen now knows to simply clear old energy via meditation, prayer, strong healthy boundaries, gratitude and forgiveness.

Sometimes she needs to specifically ask the lesson and for help to master it to release the past life energy. Stagnant energy can cause physical and/ or emotional issues when it remains stuck in your auric field for too long.

***

Fortunately, Standish's 21st century self wouldn't have nearly as large an impact on Gwen's life as he did when I was Ann Warren Little at Plimoth Plantation.

***

Gwen met Myles Standish's Future Self again a few years later at a conference where they were both exhibitors. She had asked specifically when paying for her table rental if there were preferred or assigned table locations. She learned there were not, it would be first-come, first-served with no tier pricing available.

Gwen was the first to arrive at the conference the next morning, two hours before the official opening. She walked the entire exhibit hall twice, noting where the doors opened and closed into the various conference rooms, and where the rest rooms were located. Gwen visualized the most probable traffic flow and which tables would be likely to have the best foot traffic.

Clearly the table nearest the escalator arrival and the main exhibit hall doors would be the prime spot as it was also closest to the bathrooms. She rolled her large backdrop case over to her chosen table and began to set up.

It took more than a half hour to assemble her backdrop display. It wasn't until Gwen began to arrange the table top display contents that she spotted a small sticky note with a competitor's company name.

Gwen pulled out her file and the email she'd printed stating there were no assigned tables as it was flat-fee pricing and first-come, first-served for vendor table assignments. She took a deep breath and walked the sticky note with 'Standish's' company name on it over to the farthest table from the main doors.

Gwen switched it with her company's name as she had been placed in the worst location. She completed her set-up over the next hour as the other vendors began to arrive, found their spots, and set-up wherever their company name had been noted.

Gwen visited the other booths and felt confident she had prepared well. Her booth looked great, including a large bouquet of fresh flowers from the farmer's market that she would raffle off at the end of the day.

Standish's Future Self strutted in a mere fifteen minutes before the first speaker began. He hesitated when he spotted Gwen set up in the prime spot but walked on by. She noticed his fine suit and expensive, highly polished shoes.

Gwen observed him quietly as he swaggered through the entire hall before discovering his table was the farthest from the doors. It was now also the only unoccupied table.

She heard him drop his supplies on the floor with a bang and could almost see the steam coming out his ears. He turned sharply on his heel and began striding back in her direction.

Gwen steeled herself for the conversation to come, aware that prospective customers and business partners surrounded them both and were within easy earshot.

'You're in my place,' Standish said to her, visibly trying to hold onto his temper. His face was beginning to turn red all the way to the tips of his ears.

'I was promised this spot. You need to move immediately.'

'According to the Event Coordinator, table assignment is first-come, first-served, because we all paid the same rate. I confirmed that with her yesterday,' Gwen returned evenly.

'Would you like to see a copy of the email? I have it right here,' she continued, knowing she was poking the bear.

'No, I don't want to see a copy of any damned email! I'll go find someone in charge myself,' he replied churlishly.

'You better pack up your stuff and get ready to move to the far table,' he continued, leaning over her. He was over six feet tall and she was 5'2".

'There's no time to do that,' she replied quietly. 'The conference is starting in a few minutes and my set-up takes over an hour. I'm sure the physicians will find time to visit all our tables as this is a full-day continuing education.'

Gwen walked around her table and sat down quietly to make her point. She sensed several other exhibitors watching and listening closely.

'Standish' stomped off and a few moments later she saw him setting up at the far table. She wisely kept her distance that day and wouldn't answer questions when a few fellow vendors asked quietly what had happened.

Gwen simply shrugged and replied, 'I have no idea.'

She never met him again. Gwen later learned from her Guides this was another lesson in 'standing in her power fully, without abusing it.' Lesson complete!

***

I return now to my narrative of the Mayflower's arrival at Plimoth. We learned further details as Father continued to read to us from his diary.

On December 11th, 1620, a party of Englishmen landed in Plimoth using a shallop boat they had transported aboard the Mayflower. A shallop can be sailed or rowed and had been carefully chosen for its versatility.

Everyone was so anxious to explore the coast and to disembark the Mayflower! As mentioned earlier, she was morphing rapidly from hospital ship to graveyard ship.

But the small shallop had been damaged so severely bashing about in the Mayflower's hold for several months that it took the carpenter and his assistants several weeks to rebuild her.

This caused another delay to find the best site on which to settle and to begin to build. Finally, on December 16th, 1620, Ship's Master Christopher Jones gave the order for the Mayflower to drop anchor in the shallow Plimoth Harbor. (We wouldn't find the much deeper Boston Harbor until years later.)

The exploring party chose the landing site carefully for its nearby clean, fast-running brook. This brook was an excellent source of vitally needed fresh water and fish.

We 'First Comers' might have remained in Provincetown at the tip of Cape Cod but for the lack of readily available fresh water. Plimoth was chosen as our settlement for its fresh water, not because of the fabled Plymouth Rock. I can assure you no one stepped on it to claim the area.

***

Keep a discerning mind regarding the truthfulness of so-called 'history.' History is simply a reflection of the writer's perspective and beliefs.

Be clear those in power at the time write the official history books, including the Holy Bible. A single viewpoint can accumulate tremendous power simply by being written and becoming the accepted version of events.

That does not guarantee it is truthful or accurate. I feel that way regarding much of what was written – or not written – about the many 'forgotten' or misconstrued women of the Bible, including Mary Magdalen.

Read best-selling author Julia Ingram's 'The Lost Sisterhood: The Return of Mary Magdalen, the Mother Mary and Other Holy Women' for more on this topic.

***

The abandoned Wampanoag village of Patuxet became our home. We renamed it Plimoth.

We later discovered Patuxet had been home to an estimated two thousand Native people. Why did our King say this land was unoccupied and ours for the taking?

The Patuxet Natives died so suddenly and in such great numbers from a plague there were not enough left alive to bury the dead. Bones were found above ground everywhere as the tribes dropped their bodies in a matter of weeks, if not days.

The Indians were likely infected by Spanish, French or other explorer's smallpox, a disease for which they had no immunity.

Our colonization of America would obliterate a proud, generally peaceful people who had inhabited the area for an estimated seven to eight thousand years.

In fifty short years, we unintentionally would end an entire people! Emotions are timeless, and I feel tears forming today realizing the truth of that statement.

It's a major reason why I'm grateful to share my life story as Ann Warren Little at Plimoth Plantation in the years 1623 to 1676.

***

On December 23rd, 1620 a party of our men went ashore and began gathering building materials. Work continued slowly as weather and health permitted.

During that dreadful first winter, half of our countrymen died of scurvy and other diseases. Scurvy began to present during the Mayflower's long passage followed by the confinement in the harbors, first at Provincetown and then at Plimoth.

Scurvy typically begins with bleeding gums, loosening teeth and foul breath. Ship's scurvy is caused by not getting enough fresh food. It is exacerbated if beer is rationed due to a voyage's longer-than-expected duration.

Fresh water was never available on board due to its scarcity in England. There wasn't sufficient room aboard to bring enough water, even if there had been an adequate supply.

We learned some of this from Father's letters home to England. We understood it more vividly when he shared these trials once we joined him at Plimoth.

Father referred often to his diary to fill us in accurately on the events of the previous three years. By then we had endured our own Atlantic crossing and had first-hand knowledge.

It was sobering that only half of the original settlers from the Mayflower's 102 passengers in 1620 and the Fortune's 35 passengers from the 1621 voyage were alive when we arrived aboard the Anne of London in 1623.

We learned much precious time and energy was expended trying to conceal how many had died in the New Colony. Family and friends were buried quietly in unmarked mass graves under cover of darkness.

The First Settlers were greatly concerned about appearing outnumbered, as relations with the Natives were complex from the start. The Colony was significantly outnumbered by the Natives in our early years.

Father remarked sadly that two to three people a day were dying at Plimoth Plantation during the winter of 1620. Would God spare any Pilgrims? It was a true test of our strong faith.

***

A Native named Samoset arrived in the Colony on March 16th, 1621. Samoset greeted we Englishman in our own language! This was such a welcome surprise.

Father commented that the Indians, who primarily spoke Algonquin, were much more adept at learning our language than we were at learning theirs.

Samoset was a Mohegan Native from Maine, farther to the north. Samoset returned the next day with Squanto and announced the imminent arrival of the great Wampanoag Sachem Massasoit.

Native leaders were called Sachems. Most Sachems were male, but there was the occasional female leader.

Governor Carver and Massasoit formed a treaty of peace. Squanto stayed with we English.

No one could foresee that Massasoit's youngest son, born to him late in life, would have himself legally re-named Philip decades later upon his father's death.

Nor could we envision the complex factors building over fifty years of Colonial history in America that would lead to King Philip's War in the mid-1670s.

That war would cost me – and so many others – our lives.

It would also challenge many of us in a long-lasting way at the soul level as memories are timeless.

***

In the spring of 2014 Gwen was writing 'The Flow I: Plimoth Plantation' as a novel. She was preparing to revisit Plimoth Plantation – the living history museum – and the Mayflower II replica in Plymouth to see if any additional memories presented.

Gwen mistakenly wore out her aura trying to heal all who had died during King Philip's War. There were several thousand of us. She wasn't consciously trying to heal everyone and was inefficient in her efforts, as are many new healers.

Gwen became quite ill energetically as she wasn't using her energy efficiently. She didn't know to call in God-energy, which is unlimited. Gwen unconsciously used up all her own energy and could hardly move or function the week before her eldest daughter's graduation. She felt sick and strangely weak.

Gwen requested emergency assistance from her spiritual teacher as she didn't understand what was happening.

Robin Alexis described Gwen's aura as a 'well-loved piece of clothing that has been washed so many times it's completely frayed around the edges.'

She skillfully replaced Gwen's aura and bolstered her energy in a mere five minutes. Gwen immediately began to feel better.

Her lesson was to 'put on her own oxygen mask first' and to master 'dog medicine' – to be her own best friend. Gwen had mistakenly become stuck in old saboteur war energy.

She had to learn to keep her own energy balanced while writing as her life purpose was to heal past life energy not only for herself, but to help do so for the planet. This would take her several years to master.

***

I return now to Father reading aloud from his diary. He told us that on April 5th, 1621, the Mayflower finally returned to England.

Precious few goods were available to send to begin to repay the Plantation's large financing debts. Rocks from the harbor had to be loaded on board as ballast as the ship was riding too high to be stable.

In mid-April of 1621, Governor Carver suddenly became ill and died quickly. Father told us that was when William Bradford was elected Governor. Governor Bradford would serve the New Colony brilliantly for many years.

In late September or early October of 1621, the Colonists held a harvest celebration many confuse with the first Thanksgiving. The English Planters were deeply thankful for their first successful harvest. It truly was a celebration of life.

Massasoit and an estimated ninety Natives participated, more than the remaining population of the Colony. The food was mostly game and seafood and included some of the Colony's first successful crops.

All contributed and shared equally. There were wild turkeys and our omnipresent corn in various forms, as well as four or five deer the Natives contributed to the feast.

***

Captain William Pierce would arrive via ship with desperately needed food supplies a decade later in 1631. We were close to starvation at that time after an especially challenging, bitter cold winter.

This is the more accurate origin of what most Americans celebrate as Thanksgiving. There are now growing protests regarding Christopher Columbus Day and Thanksgiving as our colonization led to the Native American's near extinction.

I believe these traditional 'American' celebrations would benefit from a new vision as our collective consciousness rises.

***

Father smiled so broadly as he shared with us the stunning beauty of that first New England fall. The leaves turned such vibrant colors, much more so than in England. He told us the gorgeous display lifted everyone's spirits as they prepared for another hard winter.

Only seven homes had been built by 1621 rather than the planned nineteen. Single men had to bunk in with the families. It was extremely crowded, and people had to get along well to survive.

Four common buildings were painstakingly constructed by hand. Our largest multi-purpose building included a cannon platform on top. This was the start to the Plantation's fort, also called a garrison.

The ground floor would become the location for everything from Sunday service to town meetings, trials, and wedding celebrations.

The original settlers built a few more boats of several types as they were greatly needed for fishing and transportation.

***

The Fortune arrived on November 9th, 1621, bringing with her thirty-five new Colonists, mostly men. This was a surprise to the original immigrants and a mixed blessing as there was not enough food for everyone.

The Colony was compromised of primarily farmers, but we had settled in a spot with poor soil which wasn't conducive to growing the beans and other seeds we brought over from England. We hadn't yet learned to rotate our crops, nor how to grow the native crops, primarily maize, later called Indian corn.

The First People would generously teach us the importance of crop rotation, to plant certain crops together to benefit two or even three types of crops planted together, and to use dead fish heads to fertilize the soil.

The region was rich in seafood and game in the early to mid-1600s, but we weren't succeeding quickly enough at adapting to fishing and hunting. These were skills in which the Natives excelled.

Another challenge was Plimoth's shallow harbor which made trading by ship difficult. Large ships had to anchor a mile or so off-shore. That was a lot of rowing back and forth to share news or to attempt a trade with us.

Father said all surely would have starved – especially during the first few difficult years – without the Indian's help.

Chapter 3

It was now my turn to narrate for Father our experience emigrating to the New World. I was twelve years old on April 12th, 1623 as I stepped aboard the Anne of London.

I practically skipped across the bouncing gangplank, despite my long skirts. I could not have been happier as we at long last set sail!

I was accompanied by my four sisters, my stepmother Elizabeth, and approximately ninety additional passengers.

We'd been waiting for this day for three long years. Our years without Father felt like an eternity to my sisters and me.

The crew was already aboard and moving about smartly, preparing to set sail. I overheard a few sailors talking about being 'rigged and ready to perfection' for the Ship Master's inspection.

We would sail from Plymouth on England's South Coast to Plimoth in the New World. We girls found it amusing that we were sailing from one Plymouth to another Plimoth.

What would the New World really be like? Would it be rustic and picturesque? When would we see Father again.

Plimoth in the New World was originally spelled with the letter 'i' by Governor Bradford in his letters back to England to differentiate it from Plymouth, England.

The spelling was later changed to Plymouth once it became part of the state of Massachusetts. This is the reason you may see Plimoth spelled both ways.

As we boarded the Anne and tried to settle into the shockingly cramped space, several of the adults quietly murmured we were going to be even more dangerously over-crowded than expected.

We had too many wives and children of the original Plimoth Plantation settlers on the cargo ship, as well as unrelated new emigrants, too.

But who could be left behind? It wasn't like you could catch the next passage later that day or the next week like in the twenty-first century. And we all so longed to reunite with our loved ones after three long years apart!

We were ready to risk it all. Some would pay with their life.

***

Our fellow passengers included Robert Bartlett. My older sister Mary would later marry Robert at the New Colony.

My Future Self Gwendolyn would recognize the soul who had been Robert at her workplace around the year 2011. She was delighted to find her former brother-in-law.

***

The Anne of London was accompanied by the Little James, originally deemed too small for passengers. The Little James was carrying what we hoped would be the best possible supplies for the Colony.

The Little James ended up being equally over-crowded with her few passengers as we simply could not squeeze aboard in such numbers while carrying our allotted one small bag per person.

Our voyage would be dangerous and uncomfortable in the extreme. Estimates ranged from two to three months' time to cross the vast Atlantic Ocean.

The Mayflower had crossed so slowly at times in 1620 it was later estimated she was averaging two miles an hour! Can you imagine? Yet we needed to travel three thousand miles of open, perilous sea.

The adults were talking so quietly – yet animatedly – among themselves as we prepared to sail that it brought us to sharp attention. Children tune in to quiet murmurings and whispers more than you think.

I overheard that risks would include disease from overcrowding, the unpredictable Atlantic and the elements, and even Pirates. I didn't care a whit. I so wanted to be with my father again and to reunite as a family!

The Anne was the last Mayflower class ship to travel from England to New England. That made Elizabeth, my sisters and me 'Original Settlers' or 'First Comers,' along with Father, who had been on the very first passage.

***

In 1623, the Anne of London traveled the Northern course of the England to America sailing route to avoid pirates. A bigger risk was falling or being washed overboard and drowning in the blink of an eye.

We learned within a few days I was blessed with good sea legs, as was Elizabeth. She wasn't especially tall and was around forty years of age on our voyage but seemed larger than life to we girls. Elizabeth had become our bedrock.

I was closest to my oldest sister Mary that lifetime. She was not so fortunate with our sailing. Mary was horribly seasick much of the voyage, as were my younger sisters.

Mary is now my youngest daughter Tanya in my current life. It's interesting Tanya had a lot of challenges with recurrent ear infections and car-sickness when she was younger – perhaps a past life carryover?

We were especially concerned about Abigail as she was only six years of age. Her listlessness combined with the greenish tint and sweaty pallor of her skin became increasingly alarming.

Conditions were starkly austere aboard the merchant supply ship as we set sail. After a fortnight, they had become grim. Living conditions were not fit for man nor beast by the time we arrived at new Plimoth.

Unfortunately, we had to be below deck most of the time. This made our seasickness significantly worse. There was not enough fresh air nor any windows from which you could gaze at the horizon and hope to quiet your equilibrium and a too frequently empty, retching belly. This added to our increasing dehydration and general misery.

We passengers had to ride in the 'tween deck, which was in-between the main deck and the hold at the bottom of the ship. It was less than five feet in height, and water leaked down on us during the numerous stormy days.

You could not move without touching someone. This type of overcrowding is extremely hard on people. Prisoners and slaves must experience this wretchedness, including being locked in as were we.

We at least were with our loved ones and knew this miserable journey was temporary. Still, we lived for the day we'd be reunited at Plimoth with our families and be free to move about!

***

Because it was so cramped, dark, and increasingly vile below deck, we were incredibly grateful when allowed to climb the ladder to take our turn above board.

Have you ever tried climbing a tricky little wooden ladder in a long skirt with multiple layers? It was not easy. We envied the boys and men their trousers.

We would go up on deck for short periods of time to get some greatly needed fresh air, light, a bit of exercise, and a sorely needed change of pace. We could only go above board when Ship's Master Pierce gave the crew the order to open the hatch to the 'tween deck when the mighty Atlantic was calm. We still had to take extreme care once topside.

Most of the time we were trapped between decks in the cargo hold, elbow to elbow, with the increasingly putrid smells. We had to deal with an increasing number of insects, rats, and other vermin as the long days and longer nights ground on. It was difficult to distinguish day from night as there were no windows or lamps of any sort.

You can understand why I was living to go topside with my family to breathe in the incredibly welcome smell of salty, invigorating sea air!

Below deck had rapidly became rank with the stench of unwashed bodies and much more foul odors.

There wasn't enough airflow for a cargo hold teeming with people packed in like sardines in a tin.

***

So many people were seasick and retching miserably. We were not able to change our clothes during the entire voyage as we had been restricted to one small bag each. Our precious bags held a single change of clothing and a crucial second pair of boots or sturdy shoes.

There was no privacy in which to change our clothes and we would have ruined our only other clothing anyway. There are no cabins or water closets on a cargo ship.

We did not have proper beds or enough basic household necessities. We were sharing one hairbrush between the six of us to save space, as an example. Head lice were spreading rapidly, contributing again to the many discomforts.

'Bathing' consisted of hoping to get top side briefly during a rainstorm. We would try to quickly wash the grime from our hands and faces the best we could, so we didn't get soaking wet and catch a chill. A chill could become deadly if it became pneumonia.

I was obsessed with the thought of taking a bath. I couldn't *wait* to wash my itchy head and long hair once we arrived in the New World! Typical girl, perhaps, but even the boys wanted to bathe after the first month or so as most of us were used to a restorative weekly bath. The adults must have been downright miserable.

***

If the decks weren't too perilous from high winds, heaving about from the waves, or heavy, lashing rains, Captain Pierce would send one of his Officers to bring some of us up on deck. We could not wait for our turn to get topside!

My favorite weather was a gentle to moderate rain. We would immediately get to a rail for balance, throw our heads back and open our mouths as wide as we could.

We were so eager to gulp some precious fresh water down our throats. First the small boys started doing this, and then the girls, and finally the adults.

There was even some much-needed laughter at these times, as we were such an amusing sight. Elizabeth said we looked like baby birds waiting for our mothers to drop food into our mouths.

The reality was we were beyond parched. Dangerously so.

***

There was no fresh water to drink those long months, or milk, lemonade, juice, or tea. Nothing we had ever had at home. We only had nasty small beer rations with every meal, even we children.

We were so desperately thirsty. Our diet consisted mainly of dried fruits, vegetables, and biscuits as there was no refrigeration to keep food fresh. There was also some dried and salted meat and fish to provide some protein.

All of it made me so extremely bone-dry, and we had only a small amount of bitter beer with which to try to gulp down our food portions. We dreamed about the taste of plentiful fresh water and for more varied, tasty food.

This tedious diet often led to illness over time, most notably scurvy. Scurvy could become deadly.

How did sailors, Ship's Masters and their Officers live like this for voyage after voyage, I wondered. It was a hard life.

I never drank beer again that lifetime. I went in boats only when there was no other choice. I'd had my fill of them from being confined aboard the Anne for so many months.

***

Since ships in our time were made from wood, Ship's Masters greatly feared fire. We were not permitted to have oil lamps or any other light source for this reason. It was always dark and gloomy in the 'tween deck.

Cargo ships have precious little ventilation and no toileting facilities, as I mentioned. We had to use slop buckets in full view of the other passengers, one bucket per family.

Those miserable buckets were always spilling. *Why* didn't they have lids?

I didn't know a slop bucket could be used in this manner – I had never seen one as we lived in the city. I thought a slop bucket was for feeding pigs or other animals. We were told not to bring chamber pots as they would be too small.

Chamber pots were so much easier to use at home. We had wooden furniture pieces they fit below. You pulled up your skirts, sat down, and the waste went down into the pot below.

At home in England, we used our chamber pots like a modern-day commode is used for disabled, elderly or post-operative patients.

It didn't work like that aboard ship. Toileting was such a trial. Our women's time of the month was an additional exercise in misery. No privacy, no way to get clean, no place to wash your soiled linens.

Elizabeth, Mary and I prayed silently to arrive safely at Plimoth Plantation before our next menstrual cycles. We were running out of clean rags to use at that time of the month.

***

Passage was a little easier for the boys and men. They quickly adopted the crew's habit of freely urinating off the back of the ship. Male passengers of all ages tried hard to get topside a few times a day to take care of business, which had the benefit of less spills below deck.

But we were a family of six females. Sigmund Freud would coin the term penis envy in the early 1900s. Yes, I had it badly during that challenging voyage. Anything to not use the dreaded slop bucket again! I had nightmares about them.

We would put that detestable tippy bucket toward the side of the ship and surround each other in a semi-circle when it was time to use it. We would make the best visual barrier we could several times a day by holding out our full skirts, touching one skirt to the next.

It was the only time I was glad it was so dismal and dark. We would each take our turn with the bucket and then hope to be able to somehow empty it before it was spilled.

Elizabeth told us cheerfully, 'This too shall pass!' She seemed to know the perfect expression or scripture for every occasion. Our stepmother truly was a marvel, a patient teacher, and our primary source of hope, along with our strong, enduring faith.

Elizabeth is now my mother in my current life as Gwendolyn Rose. She still cites the perfect adage, quotation or song lyric frequently today.

***

We Richard Warrens were crammed into a prime spot against the port side wall below deck. We were not too far from the ladder and could hope for some fresh air when the cargo cover was lashed open.

We were not too close to the ladder, either, where you were in peril of being frequently stepped on as the ship heaved about unpredictably.

People did their best to climb safely up and down the wooden ladder but sometimes stepped on the people below them. There simply was not enough room. We were piled in on top of each other like hogs for market.

***

A sunny, gorgeous day arrived suddenly without fanfare. It was a day that would change my life for hundreds of years.

No one was too seasick to climb the ladder to get some fresh air, sunshine, and exercise. We were so delighted to be topside!

The wind volume and direction felt ideal. The Anne's six canvas sails were full, as were the bonnet add-ons below. The heavy sail cloth was not snapping or billowing from sudden gusts of wind. Yet the Anne wasn't leaning like she often did when we were under full sail or lurching about like when the wind was inconsistent.

You cannot appreciate how small our ship really was on that wide-open ocean. My heart soared as it felt like we were finally making progress skimming across the endless Atlantic to reunite with Father and to see our new home!

The Little James was our only company, as was true most days – just within sight behind, if you squinted hard enough. I heard one of the sailors estimate the James was about one nautical mile back.

We enjoyed the hard glare, though it made our eyes water and we had to shade our eyes with our hands at first. Elizabeth teased us we were turning into moles from so much time in the dark and gloomy 'tween deck.

She instructed us firmly to only look forward, toward the bow or front of the ship when we were privileged to be up on deck. Her excellent reasoning was that the crew and male passengers were rather gleefully using the back of the ship as their toileting facilities with no cover. No proper young lady should witness that!

We also felt less seasick with the wind coming straight into our faces. Seeing the horizon line was heaven to settle our poor churning stomachs.

We would look slightly to the port or to the starboard, but never toward the stern. The First Officer had instructed us as to these bare basics about the ship on our first day, so we were able to follow the crew's orders as needed for safety.

***

On that rare, perfect day in May of 1623, well up in the bow at the far end of the Anne, I glimpsed a tall, well-built man. I felt a strong jolt of recognition, followed immediately by a frisson of incredible excitement.

Yet I knew I had never seen that man before, as he was unforgettable. I observed him raptly with as much discretion as I could muster.

Ship's Master William Pierce had wonderful posture. He exuded the most incredible self-confidence I had ever experienced, without seeming arrogant. Both are still true today.

William Pierce was born to be a Sea Captain, right down to his rolling gait. He was light on his feet, yet strong and steady. I could see him walk quickly and easily on the moving ship where few could. This man clearly lived at sea.

I was not surprised to learn his soul has lived many lives at sea. I believe we resided in Halifax in the 1800s when he was again a Sea Captain, that time named Andrew Myers. My name was Eliza Ann Webber, and my memories include our having a large family of nine children.

***

Captain Pierce was in the prime of life, strongly built, especially through the chest, shoulders and back. He exuded vibrant good health. I later learned Ship's Master Pierce was in his late twenties at the time.

He had a full head of hair which he combed straight back like he does in his current life. When he turned to face us and began to walk in our direction, I observed that the Captain's slightly prominent ears and hawk-like nose were all that prevented him from being classically handsome.

The Captain was masculine in the extreme. He stood out for many reasons including that he was the only man aboard that was clean-shaven, both a luxury and a commitment.

I wondered how he could possibly get water aboard to shave? I realized he must somehow use sea water and shaving cream with a straight razor, all aboard a moving ship.

Captain William Pierce was a chameleon as he spoke with the passengers and crew. He doled out what looked like crushing hand-shakes and hearty back-slaps to many of the male passengers, bowed respectfully with a flourish to the few women, and had such genuinely kind smiles for every single child.

He even kneeled or stooped down to give some of the bedraggled children gentle, encouraging hugs. This was quite unexpected from a Ship's Captain in our day, especially one so virile and strapping.

I should have seen immediately that Captain Pierce was himself a father. Would that have made any difference to our story that lifetime?

***

I saw weary faces brighten as the Ship's Master approached and spoke with them. I watched how his men subtly came to attention and were more present in their duties – no, in their entire being. He had a unique way of being fully present, energetically on his toes, just brimming with life and vitality, and inspiring the same in others.

Lance still does this today – he has such joie de vivre and determination to seize every moment fully, as it will never come around again. It was one of the things I most enjoyed about him.

It was surprising to see a man change his demeanor so quickly in the presence of men, women, and children. It was subtle, but I could sense it.

With his Officers I observed the Captain's strong intelligence and easy command. With the sailors, there was more often a rough bravado, order, or reprimand as he instantly judged what was most suitable for that seaman.

He encouraged we passengers, 'We shall be on shore in due time, when God wills it. I will make certain to reunite your families personally, to a one.'

We took heart from his unassailable belief we would sail true to our loved ones. Captain Pierce's unshakeable confidence was a living, breathing thing.

It provided much needed hope during our grueling journey, as did our faith in God.

***

Formally meeting Captain Pierce aboard the Anne of London was surreal. I couldn't drag my gaze from him as I clung to the starboard rail.

He approached the disheveled Richard Warren family as lithely as a big cat stalks its prey, despite the ship's unpredictable movements.

Captain Pierce spoke first with great respect to Elizabeth, and then with true kindness to each of my sisters in turn. I was introduced by Elizabeth last as I was hanging back, observing him – no, remembering him – re-remembering him – as if my life depended on it!

When the Ship's Master was directly in front of me, I was suddenly gazing into the deep-set green eyes and well-tanned face of a man I had known before. Many years before. In previous lifetimes. Many lifetimes – I couldn't count them all quickly enough.

The lives we'd shared flipped by in my Akashic Records Book of All Knowledge so quickly it made me dizzy. I saw those lives race by in a blur, hard and fast.

What was happening? I didn't understand I was seeing them clairvoyantly with my third eye. I wouldn't understand what the third eye was for several hundred more years.

I didn't know I was also clairaudient, clairsentient claircognizant and clairvoyant like I am again today in my current life, or what those abilities meant.

***

I was startled to hear a calm, deep voice clearly say, 'William is your primary soul mate.' What exactly was a soul mate and how could this grown-up, powerful man be mine? What did that even mean? Wasn't a soul mate someone you were meant to love and to marry?

It felt so disorienting to hear and know these things out of the blue. I had enough common sense to know no one else could feel and hear and see what I was experiencing.

I felt like I was floating partly in another world without a strong enough tether, and that I desperately needed to focus on the moment at hand. It was exhilarating, surreal, empowering, and incredibly frightening all at once.

I so wanted to remember him. I so wanted to forget him!

How could both things be true? Our energetic connection was almost too much for me.

I didn't understand I profoundly needed to ground my sacral chakra down deep into the magnetic core of Mother Earth for more support and clarity, not that it was easy to ground my energy while aboard a heaving ship.

All my energy was up in my heart chakra and higher. I could feel the energy choking my throat. My third eye was throbbing in my forehead, and my crown chakra at the top of my head felt blown wide open as I struggled to psychically process these unprecedented events.

I was only twelve years of age. I didn't know to balance my energy by moving it down to my lower chakras and from there into the mundane or lower chakras below my feet to pull up support for myself and to get more grounded.

***

I would experience this same top-heavy chakra imbalance when I woke up spiritually in the years 2011 to 2014. Fortunately, I was referred to a gifted spiritual teacher in 2013.

With time and daily practice, I learned to ground, clear and protect my energy through daily rituals and visualizations. Robin Alexis helped me begin to rebuild and strengthen my lower chakras – or major energy centers – including my root, sacral and solar plexus chakras.

Her recommendation I begin taking Vitamin B-12 was hugely helpful, too. My lifetime of headaches centered in my right temple resolved.

Robin felt I might be experiencing cumulative psychic fatigue from many lifetimes. I was grateful to feel more clear-headed, decisions became easier to make and had better outcomes.

***

Back in 1623, I was mesmerized by our Ship's Master. I waited with bated breath for what would happen next. My eyes must have been huge as time slowed down until it stood still.

When Elizabeth introduced me as her daughter Ann, the Captain made a surprising remark.

'I am especially delighted to meet you again, Ann, at long last. Clearly you are extremely special, as this ship 'The Anne of London,' is named for you!'

Again? He had just said again, we were meeting *again*. How could that be true? How could it not be true? I knew him with every fiber of my being just like I would in 2010.

He laughed so heartily and without any warning. I would instantly recognize his distinctive, abrupt bark of a laugh hundreds of years later. That unselfconscious, hearty bray was music to my ears every time we met as we seemed to share the same sense of humor.

***

Captain Pierce searched my grimy face carefully.

'You have lovely hair, Ann. Take heart. We will be back ashore soon enough, and conditions will greatly improve. Just help with your younger sisters until then, and God willing, we'll get through this long voyage together.'

My long hair was brown but turned many shades of red in the sun. It was normally shiny and bouncy, but I could not imagine what it looked like now after so long at sea?

Girls and women wore triangular white head scarves in our day for both religious and practical reasons. I nervously adjusted my head scarf.

I felt like I was about to jump out of my skin. I simply had to move, yet I couldn't move away from him. I felt pinned like a bug on display in a museum.

I couldn't manage to verbalize anything beyond a quiet and modest, 'Thank you, Captain,' as I stared down shyly at his strong-looking hands.

Pierce had clasped both of his remarkably large hands around one knee while he kneeled on the other to be eye-level with my youngest sisters.

Pierce's hands were well-weathered, like the rest of him. They bore several white scars that stood out sharply as he was deeply tanned from significant time at sea.

He wore no rings or other jewelry. I didn't realize few sailors did as it could be dangerous or even deadly to catch one's hand on something aboard ship.

The Ship's Master wore no wedding band. Captain Pierce must be a bachelor, as he was so often at sea! I smiled radiantly as my heart pulsed with overwhelming joy.

He was available – but why should that matter to me?

Once again, I heard a voice clearly say, 'William is your primary soul mate.'

***

I wouldn't know until 2013 – hundreds of years after my death as Ann Warren Little – that William's wife Jane had been wearing both halves of their gimmel puzzle ring since their wedding day. This was a new custom of our day that certain of the elite followed.

I wouldn't learn the truth of his wedding ring until my future incarnation Gwendolyn Rose and Lance, previously William Pierce, helped me get Home in 2013.

I would finally learn the truth about William Pierce's marital status from my Future Self Gwendolyn.

***

But I am far ahead of my narrative. The timeline of my soul's journey is complex as I consciously recall so many of my past lives.

I also recall a few parallel lives when my soul was incarnated in more than one body at the same time, most especially during the 1800s and 1900s. I was completing my last required stages of reincarnating on Earth before I became a Volunteer to help mankind.

***

I return now to the day I met Captain Pierce in 1623. He quite suddenly smartly bade us good day and moved on to speak with other passengers. He was always on the move.

I couldn't tear my eyes from him until we had to go below deck again, much too soon for my liking.

***

I would discover as Gwendolyn that our souls had an estimated sixteen or seventeen shared lives, including six marriages.

Despite many 'best of times' lives as friends of both genders, spouses, lovers, siblings, and one life as mother and son, my 'worst of times' were also with him.

There was too much drama and emotional load between us.

We had significant lessons to complete together, and a boatload of karma to transmute. (pun intended) I'm thankful we have completed our energetic work together.

Parting peacefully would be our last lesson. It wouldn't come easily. I would learn it only takes one to part peacefully even though it wasn't my preference at that time either. But I had learned it was best to follow my spiritual guidance as quickly as possible.

***

Until my extraordinary meeting with William in 1623, I did not know I sometimes have 'The Memory.' I am able in certain lifetimes to remember past, parallel or even glimpses of future lifetimes as time is both continuous vs. linear, as well as multi-dimensional, with everything happening at the same time.

Time is better described as a loop than a line.

I believe this ability occurs to allow greater spiritual progress. Normally there is a 'Veil of Amnesia' between incarnations to allow us the best opportunity to raise our vibration.

I was different, as are many psychics and healers who don't have the Veil and can connect meaningfully with the other side as well as some can remember their own previous incarnations.

If it's necessary to fulfill one's life purpose and soul mission, some individuals can either partially or fully open the Akashic Records storehouse of their history – past, present and even future – while incarnated.

Typically, we can do this only when we are at Home doing a life review or when planning our next incarnation.

Normally the Holy Records are accessed and interpreted for us by loving Elders, including Guides and Angels. It's rare we can directly access the Akash while incarnated, but both my friend Abby from Plimoth and I have this ability currently, as do many psychics, Mystics, Shaman, Akashic Records Readers and certain other healers.

I may have been only twelve when I re-met William Pierce aboard the Anne of London in 1623, but I did have a sense our souls were eternal. I sensed we incarnated hundreds, if not thousands of times on-planet, off-planet and in other dimensions in both human and other life forms.

This was not something I was able to discuss with many people. It was not acceptable thinking among Puritans in the 1600s – it could even be dangerous.

My older sister Mary wisely told me not to ever talk about my thoughts in this area as she rightly feared persecution.

My belief system more aligned with the Native people in America I had yet to meet. Later I would discover my numerous Native past lives, including as Wampanoag.

***

I would learn more about Captain Pierce from my fellow passengers over time. I was an excellent listener and seldom forgot anything.

William Pierce was officially living in Jamestowne, Virginia when he was Ship's Master for the Anne during our crossing. Yet he was much more often at sea.

William was born in 1595 to a father named Richard, as was I. His mother's name was Martha. The Pierces were from

Bristol, the largest port town in southwest England. Bristol traded primarily with Ireland in the early 1600s.

Captain Pierce had three brothers, both older and younger, and several sisters. His older brother John owned ships as mentioned earlier, his brother Wayne was a Sea Captain like William, and Michael went into the military.

Large families were the norm in our day.

No mention was ever made by the other passengers or crew of William having a wife or children. I blithely assumed he didn't have any, as he was too often at sea.

William didn't wear a wedding band as was our custom. But many seamen did not as they could lose a finger, a hand, or even their life if a ring or bracelet were to catch while they were working aboard ship. I was unaware of this nautical practicality.

I never thought to ask his marital status, not that it would have been a proper question from a young girl. Children were to be seen and not heard in my time.

I was only twelve and immature for my age. I was an incurable romantic, and extremely naïve by nature that lifetime, though I didn't possess that self-knowledge at the time. I trust I am now more self-aware at the eternal soul level.

Some of that awareness came with a steep price, though I regret none of it. The ride with William – as with Lance – was worth the fall. We incarnate to have experiences, and had a plethora together.

***

William's older brother John Pierce was a ship-owner as well as one of the Merchant Adventurers. The Adventurers became the financiers for Plimoth Plantation.

I heard some of the men discussing that John Pierce was pleased to entrust his brother William with looking after his financial interests. Captain William Pierce would ferry numerous passengers and many goods safely between England and America for years to come.

William became known as the 'Ferryman of the North Atlantic' for having transported so many early settlers to the New World. He was clearly an expert mariner.

The Captain seemed to sense the elements before it was humanly possible to do so, and to prepare his men and passengers the best he could as to what to expect.

Long, dreary days aboard the careening Anne of London turned into weary weeks, and finally into monotonous months. I had not enough to do and too much time to ruminate.

What did it mean that I remembered William from other lifetimes? Did he remember me at any level? Did he understand who we were to each other, had been before, or most importantly, could be again this lifetime?

I replayed endlessly that when we were first introduced up on the Main Deck, Captain Pierce said he was delighted to meet me 'again' and that it had been 'a long time.'

What did he mean by 'again'? Was there a purpose for our reunion?

Would we meet again after the Anne of London arrived safely at The New World? And what would the circumstances be?

I knew I would give anything – anything! – to see William Pierce again. It felt destined – like it had already been 'written in the stars.'

But what did that expression imply, why did I keep hearing it, and from whom? Clearly, I didn't understand the concept of the Higher Self – also known as the soul – nor of Spirit Guides.

Chapter 4

Early on the morning of July 10th, 1623, excited, joyful shouts were suddenly heard topside. I strained my ears mightily, as we were still locked below in the 'tween deck.

Sounds from above were so muffled due to the heavy wooden cargo hold door being lashed shut.

Suddenly, I could make out what the sailors were jubilantly shouting.

'Land Ho!'

I still get chills hundreds of years later recalling that joyful shouting.

Praise be to God – land had been sighted! We could hear the animated, jubilant cries of 'Land Ho!' booming and echoing all over the ship's decks, up above our heads.

'Land Ho!' was repeated many times, sung back eagerly in a growing chorus from sailor to sailor, and now down below deck through all we weary Pilgrims.

I will never forget those jubilant cries. I was not the only one who suddenly burst into unexpected tears of joy and relief. Dare we hope it was not only land that had been sighted, but the New Colony?

The seas were calm that memorable day. Captain Pierce gave the order early that morning to open the hatch down to the crammed cargo area.

We couldn't wait to get topside to peer out toward our new home. Would we perhaps be graced with a glimpse of our loved ones?

When it was finally my turn to peer through a looking glass that a kindly old sailor handed to me, at first, I could only see a few boats in the flat-looking harbor.

The patient well-worn seaman showed me where to sight on the small boats and then how to then look just past them to see the New Colony. Plimoth Plantation!

It was surprisingly tiny. My mind was racing. What would life in the New World be like? What happiness and hardships lay ahead for our family and new neighbors?

My sisters and I could not wait to reunite with Father, and Elizabeth with her husband. We were so anxious to see our home, to hope to enjoy a tasty meal with plentiful water or tea to drink, and to have a warm bath.

I could not wait to wash my filthy hair and body. We were unbearably rank.

The few little boys found our passage the easiest as they didn't care about keeping clean, although their mothers did. They instinctively understood the correlation with disease.

***

We were immensely grateful Captain Pierce and his crew had sailed true once again. It is miraculous how they navigated to that *exact* miniscule location so precisely, given the nautical instruments and maps of our day.

How did they spot those seven daub and wattle cottages from the wide expanse of the mighty Atlantic? Or was it the few little boats our men had moored in the harbor?

I was a young girl – I didn't understand how nautical navigation was accomplished.

William explained to me years later the shape of the coastline – the 'arm' of Cape Cod – is quite distinctive. They also navigated by the stars on clear nights.

William had a knowledge of astronomy, as well as mathematics – most notably trigonometry. The Ship's Masters and Officers of our day used navigational instruments such as mariner's magnetic compasses, quadrants, transverse boards and more.

***

Captain Pierce was a blur of motion as we prepared to disembark. He barked out good-natured orders to his crew, 'Prepare the looong boat, men, make lively work of it! Heave to! Prepare the loonnnng boooaaaat, post haste!'

I giggled loudly – earning a sharp look from one of the adults – as 'long boat' was a euphemism for such a small wooden boat.

Two sailors were used to row the boat as quickly as possible to shore. They sat in the middle, squeezed together hip to hip, backs toward the shore.

We could only crowd in four to six passengers in the long boat each time. We clutched our precious small bags on our laps or tucked them in tightly on top of our feet to not get our precious few possessions wet.

There was soon water in the bottom of the boat as the sailors had to climb out in the shallow waters to help carry some of the smaller children, women or bags ashore and then had to climb back in with their wet shoes or boots and pant legs. I could see some of the passengers did a little bailing while the sailors rowed.

There hadn't been room to bring a larger long boat aboard. Many trips would need to be made to transport all of us to shore.

We had to anchor about a mile out to not risk running aground as Plimoth Harbor is quite depthless. As mentioned previously, the Anne, like all Mayflower class ships, was built as a deep-drag ship to carry cargo.

We continued gathering our few possessions and queuing up in line the best we could. We could see it would be a long wait to disembark in the well-protected harbor.

We could hear Captain Pierce calling out last names alphabetically from the Ship's Rolls. And our surname was Warren. I sighed quietly to myself.

***

We would be some of the last to unload, valuable bags clutched in dirty hands. I brushed and re-plaited each of my younger sister's snarled hair with our one hairbrush as I wanted my sisters to look nice for Father.

I was also a bundle of nervous energy that needed an outlet during the several hours we waited in queue.

We lined up in the 'tween deck the best we could at first, and then finally up on the Main Deck. It was much more pleasant when we could watch our fellow passengers being rowed to shore, and to breathe in the fresh smells, including the tangy scent of the water.

Elizabeth and Mary were also trying to make us a bit more presentable for reunion with Father, but little could be done without water or a change of clothes.

41

'We will bathe soon enough, at long last,' Elizabeth commented encouragingly.

We were beyond filthy. I prayed to never see a rat, vermin, or most especially a slop bucket again. We were delighted to leave that hated item aboard.

I pity the sailors who had to swab out the 'tween deck. No amount of hazardous duty pay was enough for that odious task.

***

It took much of the day to disembark the Anne of London. Sailors took their turn at the long boat oars, rowed almost a mile to shore and then returned briskly for the next group. When the sailors tired, they were immediately replaced by two other crewmen.

We filled the long boat as much as was prudent each time. She was riding so low at times I wondered if she would swamp. We were thankful for the calm waters in the harbor that memorable summer day, or the rowing would have taken even longer.

God forbid if we would have had to wait for better weather – I would have self-combusted from excitement!

Finally, it was our turn to board the long boat. We squeezed in as a family by placing Abigail on Mary's lap, and balancing Sarah on Elizabeth's.

We thanked Captain Pierce profusely as he said his farewells to each of us in turn as we were helped to disembark the ship.

He knew every single passenger's name without hesitation, even the children, which I found extraordinary. Clearly he had studied the Ship's Rolls well, and learned to match each of our names with our faces.

We climbed down another tricky long ladder into the gently moving long boat as the sailors worked to steady it. Long skirts again were not our friend. We had to take great care to not slip and fall into the boat or the water, or to twist our ankles.

The sailors carefully handed down our belongings once we were in the small shallop. This allowed us to use both hands to descend the swaying wooden ladder and to try to manage our skirts.

Once settled in the long boat, I was torn with looking ahead toward the Colony and stealing looks back over my shoulder at Captain Pierce.

William stood solidly on the deck, beaming from ear to ear. He looked so incredibly happy and proud.

I could hear his charming, sincere 'Fare thee wells,' as he helped the last few families off the Anne of London.

***

Elizabeth reprimanded me a bit sharply to stop twisting around in my seat. She told me to behave like a young lady and to set an example for my younger sisters.

I sneaked a last look at William and clearly heard, 'Never fear – you will see your soul mate again.'

I couldn't stop smiling to know that. And now we would reunite with Father and see our new home and settlement!

***

I switched my attention to getting to Father as quickly as possible, unconsciously leaning forward in the small boat.

We could now see a few small grey clapboard cottages with steeply pitched roofs, several larger buildings set back more from the water, and various kinds of wooden boats. The boats were bobbing gently in the wide, calm harbor. Everything came into sharper focus as we drew closer agonizingly slowly, stroke by stroke.

We soon learned what it had been like to painstakingly build the structures and boats by hand in the previous three years.

Our men were primarily growers, now called farmers, not carpenters. This was no small accomplishment with no finished building supplies and so few tools.

Most of the men had been working in the fields when we arrived. We discovered later many of them had thrown precious tools aside with the excitement of a ship arriving, especially one they so hoped had family aboard from England!

There had been no way to know when we would arrive, and that we were safe, though of course our families had been praying for us daily, as we did for them. You couldn't easily call or text like in current times, and few remembered how to use their telepathy like we did at Home once they had incarnated into a dense human body.

I ran ahead with unusual wild abandon and greeted Father first! I will never forget the joy of that first hug and words exchanged with him.

He then hugged each of my sisters and Elizabeth in turn, each of us for the longest time. Three long years of separation melted away in an instant.

***

Gwen relived this moment vividly during her 2013 Quantum Healing Hypnotherapy session when she spoke as me – as Ann Warren – for over an hour. Her voice on the recording is remarkable for the pure joy – mixed with happy tears – as she described reuniting with her father.

I am thrilled Richard's soul is my father again today. He remains remarkably handy and can repair or build anything.

***

Copious tears of joys were shed as Father took us to our simple home. He and several of the men worked so hard to build it during that first harsh winter of 1620, using local trees. They had no finished building supplies with which to work – one didn't just drive over to Home Depot or the local lumber yard.

The structure was more of a cottage or cabin when compared to our much larger, more comfortable home in the Greater London area.

Plantation homes were made of narrow slats of wood, using daub-and-wattle construction, and had steeply thatched roofs to naturally shed snow during the harsh winters. Otherwise the roof could collapse or require snow removal. No one had time or energy for that task, plus it would have been dangerous.

I learned immediately we were extremely fortunate to have our tiny home all to ourselves. The common buildings were turned essentially into dormitories every night for all the single men. Some of the men who weren't yet married had to bunk in with families as there were only eleven buildings in total when we first arrived.

I loved the location of our home. It was exactly what I would have chosen. It was the first home on the right as you came up from the water, or the last on the left if you were coming down from the meeting house fort.

***

Gwen recognized the Warren home immediately when she visited the Plimoth Plantation living museum in 2014. Yet she hadn't known if there would even be a Warren house represented at the current day Plimoth Plantation as that information is not listed on the website.

She had trouble entering the Myles Standish home before she even knew which home it was – and the homes are not labeled. Such is the nature of energy – it can cross all time and space until we learn to release it, and to master associated lessons such as forgiveness.

***

I held my breath as we entered through our small front door. Taller teens and adults had to bend down to enter our simple Colony homes. I looked around at what was essentially a single room.

Father commented to Elizabeth that Colony homes were built to measure about twelve to fifteen feet on each side. The floor was packed dirt, which had been difficult to level.

There was a large open hearth for cooking as well as our only heat source. I saw a few cooking utensils, pots, pans and dishes stacked neatly in the far corner to the right.

There was a bucket of sand Father explained was for fire safety. He showed us how to throw it on a fire to smother it were it to blaze out-of-control. We watched solemnly and learned what to do in case of a cooking fire emergency.

This was survival lesson number one. There would be many more to come.

There were a few small windows covered with parchment. Father told us the windows could be shuttered as necessary. The windows did not have glass as it was not available to us at that time like many other things we once considered necessities.

There was a good-sized table to my left, with a mixture of cleverly built small chairs and stools that he explained served multiple purposes. That simple table would be used for so many things. We quickly learned even a table was a rare luxury at the Colony.

Most families had a sawhorse and plank and would put it away after every meal to save space. That multi-use table would become one of the happiest places in our home, along with being together in front of the open hearth for a few moments on the many damp or cold days and nights.

***

I blew out my breath audibly on a long, contented sigh. I hadn't realized how shallowly I was breathing.

This was our new home. And we were all together!

We were blessed to have our entire immediate family reunited. Some women and children arrived to find their husband or father, or other loved ones had passed on and word had not yet reached them.

What devastating news to bear especially after that long and difficult ocean passage.

I shuddered visibly when I heard the keening cries from several women and children who were suddenly without their family. What would happen to them?

Some of the men at the Colony were learning the same, that not all had survived our perilous ocean journey. Some had lost their wife or child, or even multiple family members at the eleventh hour of being reunited.

I listened closely to ensure all were being comforted before returning my full attention to my own family. I would pray for not only my family that night and every night thereafter, but for our Plantation neighbors and friends.

Thus, the fabric of the Colony wove tight.

***

Clearly, we would need one another more than ever before to survive such an isolated location. I had not understood how tiny and remote the Plantation would be.

I had envisioned something more quaint, charming, rustic and perhaps even jolly.

Yet I was clear there was no turning back – we would be here for the rest of our days, until God called us Home.

We continued exploring our home. There was a high bed for our parents in the far right-hand corner of the main room. The bed had a lovely patchwork quilt Elizabeth had made a few years earlier.

Father had brought the quilt aboard the Mayflower in the single small chest he was allowed. He also brought the iron cooking utensils and a few pots, pans and dishes that would serve our family well for many years.

It didn't concern us that our home was a tiny cottage. We were together again. I couldn't stop smiling!

I was gratified to see a small chamber pot chair in one of the tiny back bedrooms Father had painstakingly added in a second round of construction. No more slop bucket to spill, and to be forced to use with no privacy – I was elated, as that had been one of the hardest parts of the ocean passage for me.

Father explained most homes had sleeping lofts that were accessed by ladder. I'd had my fill of ladder-climbing aboard ship and was thrilled we had the rare luxury of two tiny bedrooms at the back of our little home.

I spotted a portable washtub tucked under the foot of my parent's bed. I realized their bed was built higher than the norm to allow for storage underneath as our homes were so tiny.

This would be called a Captain's bed at sea. It would have pull-out storage drawers underneath. Most sailors had narrow single bunks they had to take turns with, depending who was on duty.

This practice later became called hot-bunking, first on ships and then on submarines as the bunks were essentially always occupied and didn't have time to cool between occupants.

I could not wait to be allowed to place the washtub in a back bedroom for privacy when it was my turn for my first bath in three months. My head was so itchy I suspected lice or other vermin, my long hair smelled absolutely rank and my body had never been so filthy in my entire life.

We were delighted to take turns learning how to haul water and heat it for one another. I'll never forget the pleasure of that first bath after months at sea!

We had a precious bar of soap to share. Elizabeth even found some lavender to break off and sprinkle into our bath water to help us get squeaky clean.

***

Meal times together as the Richard Warren family were the highlight of my day. Father's ears must have been flooded from the excited chatter of five young girls after three years without us.

Normally children were 'to be seen and not heard,' meaning permission had to be given by an adult for a child to speak. But for the first few days while alone at home, our parents allowed us to break that convention as there was such great joy in becoming fully reacquainted.

Father could hardly take in how much we had all grown. Our table was crowded, but happy, with meal times first for seven, then eight, and finally nine.

Our younger brothers Nathaniel were born in 1624 and Joseph in 1626. We never considered them half-brothers. We were one loving family.

Elizabeth had become our mother during our three years alone with her in London while Father was in the New World. No disrespect was intended toward our birth mother, whom we prayed for every night.

***

Elizabeth was my stepmother at Plimoth Plantation and is now my mother. She even has the same first name.

My birth mother as Ann Warren is now my stepmother. My belief is it is common for our soul group family to incarnate with us many times in varying roles.

I found one of my younger brothers when I recognized him in a Facebook group by his name and energy. He runs a healing center this lifetime.

***

Upon the Anne of London's arrival, major changes were instituted to daily life at the Colony. Everyone had been growing corn and all other crops together to share equally. The men worked the fields, and the few women remained at home with their children.

But in 1623 with our arrival doubling the population to about one hundred and eighty people, Governor Bradford and the other Elders made the choice to allow each family to also grow our own food in private plots behind our homes. Each family would be allowed to eat, sell or trade what they produced privately.

Productivity soared as women were now working the fields with their children along, tending the long rows of corn, or working in their gardens and with the livestock. We purposefully grew different crops than our neighbors to be able to trade food and have more variety in our diet.

Over time we tended to approximately one hundred and fifty acres of corn as a Colony. We learned to grow native crops of maize, squash, pumpkins, beans and potatoes. We also had some success with Old World crops of turnips, carrots, peas, wheat, barley and oats.

Colonials and Natives alike embraced our successfully learning to brew beer at Plimoth Plantation. Beer, ale and cider were referred to as 'English manufacture.'

We began to raise cattle, goats, sheep, rabbits, and hens. There were a few dogs and cats in the Colony. We first imported and then bred a precious few horses.

Over time, we sorted out who was best as a farmer. A few of our men learned to fish or hunt more productively, though we would never match the Natives in these endeavors as they had perfected them over thousands of years.

Many women and children became proficient at finding and picking berries, fruits, roots and edible grasses, and at digging clams. My favorite task was to dig clams, as I loved being by the water. Solitude was a rare treat, and I could most easily hear my Guides by the water.

Most appealing of all, I could discreetly watch for ships while clam-digging and still do my share of the work. I watched for William for years, both from by the waterfront and from atop the big rock near the trading post.

***

Decades later I would become confused after my death, and would continue watching for him – waiting, always waiting, yearning to understand what had happened to William.

Over time I desired only closure. William had said he would come back for me – but when?

I failed to fully recognize him as the soul who had been Ship's Master William Pierce until 2013, though we incarnated together in the interim more than once.

***

Our food supply and shelter standpoint improved as the years rolled by, season by season. Yet an especially harsh winter or fire could change things quickly.

A few of the more affluent families had servants who primarily helped work in the fields and outdoors, or with the heavier or more unpleasant housework such as hauling water and emptying and cleaning the chamber pots.

I was thrilled slop buckets were now only used to feed our livestock once I debarked the Anne of London. Life is certainly more challenging when you don't have running water, but we were blessed to have ample potable water to drink and cook with, and for limited bathing, laundry and housekeeping purposes. We also had enough clean water for the precious crops and livestock that sustained us.

***

We passengers from the Mayflower, the Fortune, the Anne of London and the Little James comprised the Old Comers, or original settlers. We had risked the most and often received preferential treatment in later colony land and financial transactions. This led to resentment at times.

In 1623, Father received acreage in the Division of Land. In November of 1623, shortly after our arrival, a fire destroyed several of the buildings at the Colony.

Some Colonists lost both their homes and possessions and had had no choice but to return to England on the next supply ship. We simply did not have enough housing or supplies to share with them.

In 1624, a religious controversy centering on the Reverend John Lyford resulted in large numbers of people leaving Plimoth. Some returned to England or journeyed to other areas of New England.

We once again had barely sustainable numbers at the Colony. Times were exceptionally hard.

People require drinkable water and clean air in addition to food and shelter and a reasonable temperature to survive.

***

Let's not forget the 2016-2017 controversy over the DAPL (Dakota Access) oil pipeline at Standing Rock, North Dakota.

'Water is Life' is much more than a slogan.

My belief is Standing Rock and other key energetic tipping points are crucial to sustaining life on our beautiful planet.

I conclude this topic with a quote from Alanis Obomsawin, an Abenaki from the Odanak Reserve 70 miles NE of Montreal as written in Ted Poole's 1972 edition of 'Conversations with North American Indians.'

'Canada, the most affluent of countries, operates on a depletion economy which leaves destruction in its wake. Your people are driven by a terrible sense of deficiency.

When the last tree is cut, the last fish is caught, and the last river is polluted; when to breath the air is sickening, you will realize, too late, that wealth is not in bank accounts and that you can't eat money.'

It's not too late to change, including to reverse global warming. How can you lighten your footprint on the planet, beginning today?

***

I return once again to the year 1620. Captain Myles Standish had arrived aboard the Mayflower with my father on that first crossing. Standish was the military man entrusted with the security of the New Colony.

He is considered a brave hero by many. My experiences and memories differ.

Standish made a disastrous raid at Wessagusett early in the Colony's history. He slaughtered several Natives in their wigwam after tricking them he was there peacefully.

Standish also fired the first shot at the First Encounter when we initially landed and were exploring in December of 1620.

The Wessagusett killings understandably frightened the Natives. Word spread quickly of the white man's treachery and violence.

Many fled their settlements to avoid us. Sadly, they starved over time, or died from diseases picked up in the swamps.

***

Standish's behavior led to many issues with re-establishing trading and our relationship with the Natives. I believe his behavior created enemies. I feel he did as much harm for the Colony as he helped with our – quote – 'protection.'

Everyone needed to contribute in a meaningful way for the Colony to survive as our numbers were so small. Helping with my younger sibling's care and education, our own garden and livestock, and cooking and cleaning wasn't enough. I needed to contribute more even as a teen girl.

We didn't have formal schools outside the home for many years to come. I showed no affinity for farming or for fishing as I could barely stand to get in a boat after my Atlantic crossing.

But I could bring order to things easily, knew how to inventory goods, calculated sums rapidly and accurately, communicated well, and was congenial with most people.

These were the skills I brought to what would become Plimoth Plantation's trading post.

Father initially set up the little post. He taught me the basics as he had been both a grower and a merchant in England. I had always loved his storefront back home, and now I would help build one in the New World!

This was truly exciting for me and would immeasurably broaden my world.

Seeing a teen-aged girl working in the trading post vs. an armed adult male must have been reassuring to the first Natives who bravely, tentatively approached us to re-establish trade after Standish's brutal, ill-advised raid.

We had to build the trading post outside the Colony's palisade fence for any Natives to be willing to approach and enter the small wooden building as they understandably feared ambush. We also built outside the fence for the convenience of the Ship's Masters, the Officers and the few sailors who sought us out.

***

I spent much of my time working in that tiny trading post. This provided me with unusual freedom for a girl my age in Colonial America.

We traded mostly with the Natives, their beaver skins for our Indian corn. We then traded the furs with Ship Masters for English and other European goods that we couldn't produce ourselves at the Plantation.

We were even able to trade with our own Ship's Master William Pierce. The trading post became my rendezvous point with William over time. This was unintentional at first.

My wise and protective parents must have considered me safe working at the trading post or I would not have been there unarmed, outside the palisade fence. So why did we need that fence which took so many of our precious resources to build and to maintain?

Were there really that many wild animals that could harm a human being or our livestock? Or was this more about living as an armed camp from the start and as a fear-based society. Were we already marching toward war with the

Natives due to their different customs, language and skin color?

***

What if man's ultimate journey is to truly re-remember and embrace we are all ONE? Souls look exactly alike in our pure soul form. We're all beautiful pure White Light energy, and there is no duality, no separation from Source.

Reuniting with her soul group was one of Gwen's favorite moments during her comprehensive Life-Between-Lives hypnotherapy session in 2012. The joy she felt in that reunion was tremendous! Every soul looked exactly alike, yet she knew exactly who each one was by their unique energy signature.

***

Our trading as a Colony became so proficient over time we squeezed out the French who had been previously trading with the Natives. We now had home court advantage.

It must have alarmed the Natives that we had clearly settled permanently. They worked to adapt to us as there was no choice, as we did to them.

In 1626, we built our first large trading house at Aptucxet on the southwest side of Cape Cod. We traded from there with the Natives of both Cape Cod and Narragansett Bay.

On May 22nd, 1627, the colony began to divide its major assets, beginning with our livestock. This Division of Cattle was like the Division of Land in 1623. The Division of Cattle listed most of the Plantation inhabitants by name and is an important piece of history.

***

Our livestock was crucial to our survival as it would become again in my life as Jesse Applegate, an Oregon Wagon Train Leader. Applegate led the Cow Column west in 1843 for a grueling two thousand mile, four-month journey from Missouri to Oregon. We walked it primarily on foot, not on horseback or in the wagons as the terrain was too rugged.

***

Almost everyone in the New Colony was taught how to read and to write at home, primarily so we could read the Bible for ourselves. We preferred the Geneva edition of the Bible, first published in English in 1560.

The translation and footnotes of the Geneva Bible were made by early Calvinists and were more trustworthy to us than the later King James Bible whose translation and footnotes were written by the Anglican Church.

We sang only actual Biblical psalms as we did not believe in singing hymns that were not direct Biblical texts. Henry Ainsworth, who was from an English Separatist church in Amsterdam, wrote the psalm book we used at Plimoth.

We sang unaccompanied by an organ. This is difficult to accomplish in a tuneful or pleasing manner.

***

William Brewster was our Church Elder. We had several deacons and a deaconess. We honored the Sabbath by not performing any labor on Sunday other than necessary livestock tending and minimal garden watering and housework.

Sunday was spent in full-day worship. We wore what was referred to as our 'Roast Meat Clothes' in England because of the habit of serving a beef roast with vegetables for Sunday dinner. This clothing later became called one's 'Sunday Best.'

Our church was intended to be organized around five officers: pastor, teacher, elder, deacon and deaconess. None of the five offices was considered essential to the church, fortunately, as we didn't have enough people to fill these roles.

The Pastor was an ordained minister whose responsibility was to see to the religious life of the community. John Robinson was to have been Plimoth's pastor, but he was not able to get to America before his death in Holland in 1625.

The teacher was also an ordained minister who was responsible for the instruction of the congregation. We never had anyone to fill that position. You need to fully appreciate how small our numbers really were.

The Elder was a lay-person responsible for our church government. William Brewster was our Elder for the Plimoth church.

Church deacons collected offerings and attended to the needs of the poor and elderly. John Carver and Samuel Fuller were both deacons.

The deaconess attended the sick and poor, and often played the role of midwife for the congregation. Bridget Fuller was Plimoth Plantation's deaconess.

Our church was the bottom floor of the town's fort. The top floor held six cannons and a watchtower as part of defense preparations. The fort also functioned as our meetinghouse and was the location for court sessions and town meetings.

I married Thomas Little at the meetinghouse in a civil ceremony on April 19th, 1633. Weddings were not religious events in our day at the Plantation.

***

I had trouble explaining to my hypnotherapist what the 'church' looked like when she asked me that question during my first Quantum Healing Hypnotherapy session. The meetinghouse was such a multi-purpose building.

Animals could be housed there on occasion. This threw me off to see as Gwen in 2013, remembering being Ann in 1633, and being asked if I had a church wedding? My left-brain interrupted abruptly to question why an animal would be in a church, other than perhaps during a Nativity scene.

But the meetinghouse served as both church, meeting hall and garrison and occasionally housed some livestock. It is important for people to simply state what they see, feel and experience during a past-life regression and to not judge or question it.

My memory of animals sometimes being housed in the building where I was married at the Plantation was correct, though it made no sense to me initially in 2013 until I did some research and validated my memory.

Trust your first instinct is the lesson, and act on it timely.

***

A couple would register their betrothal three weeks before the wedding. A wedding ceremony would include witnesses chosen by the couple going before the magistrates in a town hall or other suitable public building.

A wedding was typically followed by a wedding banquet.

Church buildings had no significance and were intentionally kept drab and plain, with no religious depictions, crosses, windows, fancy architecture or icons to avoid the sin of idolatry.

We didn't have time or energy to invest in those things for years to come. More importantly, they didn't fit our beliefs.

Governor Bradford's posing for a formal portrait when visiting Europe became the best example of Colonial period clothing.

Gwen was gratified to read a description of Bradford's stark black and white formal attire late in 2013. It was exactly what she described during her June 2013 hypnotherapy session as what her husband Thomas Little wore for his wedding with her when she was Ann Warren.

***

We honored only two sacraments at Plimoth Plantation, baptism and the Lord's Supper. The other sacraments of the Church of England and Roman Catholic Church included confession, penance, confirmation, ordination, marriage, final confession and last rites.

These were considered inventions of man, without a scriptural basis. Therefore, we did not follow them.

Prayer was encouraged to be spontaneous rather than scripted. You were expected to pray from your heart, not to cite long memorized prayers.

***

Marriage ceremonies were performed by civil magistrates rather than by a religious leader. Marriage was a contract, mutually agreed upon by a man and a woman. It was created by God for the benefit of man's spiritual life.

Marriage was considered important for two reasons: procreation of children to increase God's flock, and to avoid the sin of adultery.

Our pastors taught that the important characteristics to find in a spouse were godliness, and similarity in age, beliefs, estate, disposition, inclinations and affections.

I find 'similar characteristics' still a good model today but I no longer believe in the artificial limit of 'a man and a woman,' nor for the need for procreation in such a crowded, polluted world. That may change if we lose our ability to easily reproduce as has occurred on other planets.

Most Plantation men married for the first time in their mid-twenties, and women around the age of twenty. The average life span of a man was into his seventies, and women only into our sixties due to the stresses of extensive childbearing.

Women gave birth to an average of five to six children or more approximately every two years, just like my birth family with five girls approximately two years apart.

An estimated twenty percent of women died in childbirth. Infant mortality was twelve percent the first year of life. All infants were baptized as we believed in original sin.

***

Widows and widowers most often remarried within six to twelve months due to societal and economic pressures. Many men would have two or three wives over their lifetime due to childbed fever being so frequently fatal.

Families often took in children from other families if they had been orphaned or there weren't enough resources to care for them. We didn't require orphanages – we took care of our own community.

Children were expected to move out as young adults, to marry, and to establish their own household. They often lived quite close to one or both sets of parents.

***

Women in the New Colony had significantly more extensive property and legal rights than in England. A woman could not be disinherited by her husband. Any child born of a legal union would inherit.

There were even some prenuptial agreements that protected women's properties in second and subsequent marriages. Women occasionally served on juries.

Burial of the dead was also a civil matter. We buried our dead in churchyards, over time, after those first few chaotic years at Plimoth. We didn't do so at first as we didn't have a churchyard available. More importantly, we were trying to hide the high number of our dead loved ones from the Natives.

***

Although we continued our explorations of Cape Cod and other surrounding areas for many years, we stopped everything and stayed in camp on Sundays to honor the Sabbath. We held all-day services as I mentioned earlier.

My use of the word 'camp' is purposeful. You must understand Plimoth was always an armed camp at some level for the more than fifty years I lived there.

Puritans did not celebrate Christmas and Easter as we believed those occasions were invented by man to memorialize Jesus Christ. They are not prescribed by the Bible or celebrated by the early Christian churches and therefore we did not consider them Holy Days.

This became divisive as some of the settlers strongly believed those days should be celebrated as important religious holidays. My point is even our small, closely-knit group had religious differences.

***

We worshipped at the fort-meetinghouse in the early years at Plimoth. Every man and boy old enough to handle a weapon was required to bring a musket or firelock to church. You could be fined twelve pence for failing to do so.

We would assemble to the beat of a drum by Captain Myles Standish's door. His home was the closest to the fort. It's the first on your right as you face the water.

This illustrates what a large role Captain Standish played at the Colony as did his insistence the men build a palisade fence all around the Colony in our earliest years of settlement. I reiterate this set the tone for us being an armed camp.

Standish ordered us about as if we were his chattels, especially women. I greatly disliked that bombastic little man! He was quite the arsworm to me, which I think will translate easily to your modern English.

Standish was so short of stature at approximately 5' 2" that he had to shorten his sabre by six inches or it would drag on the ground. The average man in our day was about 5'7" tall, and certainly some were taller.

I'm certain that galled 'Captain Shrimp,' which is the unkind name several of us called him behind his back. I started that rude name which was not one of my finer moments.

I disagreed strongly with his treatment of the Natives as did many moderates at the Colony. I felt Standish created as many enemies for Plimoth Plantation, if not more, than he 'protected' us from.

Over time, Standish became part of the fuse that lit the powder keg that led to King Philip's War. I had a closer, more friendly relationship with the Natives than most at the Colony as I knew many of them well on an individual basis from my years working in the trading post.

I was always treated with respect and kindness, even deference, by the many peaceful Indian men with whom I traded. Some became my friends both during my life and many more did after my death.

Certainly, some tried to drive a hard bargain, as did I. That is part of the merchant process. But both sides worked to be fair in our trades as these were lifetime relationships for most of us. Perhaps that makes it easier to always behave with integrity. Reputations lived on for a lifetime.

***

You may be surprised to learn many of us read a variety of books, plays and poems at the New Colony, especially during the long, dark evenings. We often read or sewed when we were unable to easily work outside or to maintain our simple homes. Our habit was for one of us to read aloud while other family members sewed or quietly did other hand work that didn't require a lot of light.

We read more than just the Bible. My Future Self Gwendolyn had to verify that in several historical documents as she didn't believe what I told her about my reading Shakespeare. Initially she resisted including that as part of my life's story in this book.

Gwen has since learned to trust she hears her Spirit Guides exceptionally well, and to just 'go with the flow.'

The early probate records of Plymouth Colony occasionally provide an inventory of book titles owned by the deceased at the time of their death. Elder William Brewster had several hundred books in his personal library. Not all were of a religious nature.

Books were treasured possessions passed on from household to household through the Colony and returned carefully to its owner. I waited patiently for my turn to read William Shakespeare's famous thirty-six plays.

Shakespeare's 'First Folio' was published in 1623. A treasured copy made its way to America on a supply ship with a passenger a few years later and was passed around the Colony.

I eventually received my own copy as a special gift from William. I treasured it for a lifetime.

The First Folio is organized into three genres: comedies, tragedies, and histories. My sisters, closest friends and I would read the various play parts aloud and act them out on those long, dark New England fall and winter evenings. Sunset came at around 4:15 p.m. on our shortest days.

We were delightfully silly at times as we read Shakespeare! We would have only a little lantern light until daybreak at around seven a.m. on the shortest days of the year. Life was quite different before electricity and running water.

Chapter 5

There was a profound reason I so loved to read Shakespeare as Ann Warren.

My Future Self Gwendolyn was initially highly skeptical when shown she had been married to Will Shakespeare. It took time for her to accept she was Anne Hathaway immediately before she incarnated as Ann Warren.

Gwen was watching an episode of Dr. Who on television with her youngest daughter when the main characters time-traveled to the time of Shakespeare. She was stunned to begin to vividly recall her own life with William Shakespeare.

Gwen clairvoyantly saw what I can best describe as a split-screen on their large flat-screen television at home that day. The Dr. Who episode was playing on the left, and Gwen saw her own life as Anne Hathaway with Will Shakespeare on the right.

Initially, she rejected this information from Spirit. Gwen was especially uncomfortable to be shown another famous, historical or Biblical past life as she has others and wanted to ensure her ego was well-balanced and not just making up fanciful tales.

She meditated after the program was over to reach clarity. Gwen grounded and protected to begin meditating and took a few slow deep breaths to seat herself firmly in her body and to raise her vibration and frequency.

Gwen told her Spirit Guides, 'Thank you for showing me I may have been Anne Hathaway. Please show me validation so I know I'm understanding you correctly. I need to understand the purpose, as I feel there needs to be a reason for a past life to present – is there past life energy I need to release?'

She was clairvoyantly shown many images of herself and Lance talking about Shakespeare's many plays, movies they'd seen about him both at the theater and at home, and a very special summer evening when they attended a Shakespeare play in the park together.

Gwen was shown the brown battered cover of Shakespeare's collected works she had read in college. She remembered the weight of that heavy book in her light mauve nylon backpack.

She hadn't remembered her backpack color or that huge book until that moment – it had been more than thirty years. Why were these images suddenly returning?

Gwen's skeptical response was 'Just because we both like Shakespeare and are familiar with his works doesn't mean we lived in his lifetime, let alone as Will and Anne.'

'You'd need to show me more for me to accept this as a past life. It could be an archetype, or fantasy, or I'm simply wrong. But I know archetypes can be useful – what more would you like me to know to help my life now?'

She didn't hear more at that time, only sensed her Guides smiling. Gwen thanked them and ended her meditation.

**

Gwen was driving home from work the next day when she heard a sudden urgent 'Look, look!' from Spirit as she entered her neighborhood. She looked around sharply to make sure there wasn't another car, person or animal to avoid.

Her eye was drawn immediately to her neighborhood's Tiny Little Library. Gwen braked hard to park just past the wooden trading box by the side of the road. The library box wasn't much larger than a mailbox.

She got out of her car and muscle-tested was Spirit guiding her to look in the library box? Gwen had never opened it before.

She got a strong yes from muscle-testing, and then clearly heard 'Shakespeare!'

Gwen took a deep breath as she stood in front of the neighborhood book box and stated her intent clearly.

'Please show me definitive proof if I was indeed Anne Hathaway, married to Lance as Will Shakespeare.'

Gwen took another deep breath and opened the box. A battered paperback copy of 'Hamlet,' by William Shakespeare, fell out unexpectedly and landed face-up on her right foot.

She burst into surprised tears as she gaped at Hamlet lying on the ground, knowing she had indeed lived a life as Anne Hathaway.

***

Strong sudden emotion is often a confirmation of a past life, as emotions are timeless. Our souls have an eternal memory at the cellular level, across all space and time.

She picked up the dog-eared copy carefully, sensing it had belonged to a male teenager who had been heartily relieved to be done with that portion of his English class.

Gwen mused how convoluted time could be as her own high school days in the 1970s felt like forever ago, yet the 1500s suddenly felt like yesterday.

She walked slowly to her car clutching the battered copy of Hamlet. Her Guides commented she needed to complete the trade with a book from 'the man who used to be Shakespeare.'

Gwen had taken a book, so she needed to place one in the book exchange in return. This was an energetic trade.

She looked at her own bookcase immediately upon arriving home, wondering what she could possibly give from 'the man who used to be Shakespeare?'

Gwen saw the book Spirit was referring to immediately. She had two copies of Lance's first book.

Gwen placed a copy in the book box on her way to work the next morning, knowing it would find its way to the right person. There must be some information in Lance's book that someone in her neighborhood needed.

She smiled happily – Spirit at work!

***

There's been much debate who wrote the thirty-six plays and other works attributed to William Shakespeare.

What if many men have been Shakespeare at different times and have written one or two or more of his works?

This would account for why some of his plays are so different from others, more so than is the norm of a writer progressing through their career. It would also answer how one man could possibly write so many incredible plays in one lifetime and make such an enduring impact on the English language.

Gwen heard her Guides say Lance had written 'The Taming of the Shrew,' in addition to 'Hamlet,' and possibly a few other works. They commented 'He was a prolific Shakespeare,' fitting with her theory multiple men may have written Shakespeare's many works during their various incarnations as Will Shakespeare.

She meditated to ask again if Lance wrote 'Taming of the Shrew' when he was Will? Gwen heard immediately before she had even finished asking the question, 'You know he did. You were there.'

Doubting Thomas Gwen asked for more proof. She was immediately shown the image of them at the park a few summers earlier, enjoying the free performance of 'The Taming of the Shrew.'

She was shown what had occurred after that play, as detailed in 'The Flow I: Plimoth Plantation' (the upcoming novel).

Her Guides told Gwen, 'Now you understand what the energy was on that special day. Just enjoy it and be comfortable sharing it with others. Magic in the air is rare. One would be wise to seize that NOW moment immediately as it may not come around again on the wheel of time.'

***

Gwen asked for the lessons from that life. She knew they'd had an unconventional marriage with Anne being older than Will, and that their first-born had arrived 'prematurely' six months after their hasty marriage. (She had been pregnant at the time.)

They had also lived apart for much of their marriage. Will needed to be in London to earn a living to support his family. They agreed it was best she remain in their country home with the children as London was not an especially safe or healthy place at the time.

Gwen didn't hear anything more, so completed her meditation and expressed her gratitude.

***

A half hour later, she checked her Facebook feed. Immediately a meme popped up in celebration of what would have been Shakespeare's 450th birthday! She'd had no memory of his date of birth.

It felt like strong synchronicity. Many would consider that another confirmation of that lifetime. Gwen clearly heard her Guides speak as she continued to stare at the meme.

'Lance wrote The Taming of the Shrew when he was Will. He wrote Hamlet, too, to honor your son that died.'

They had a son that died? Perhaps she could verify that on-line. Gwen immediately googled. She hadn't known consciously that the Will Shakespeares had a son named Hamnet and that Hamnet had a twin sister.

Hamnet had died of unknown causes at the age of eleven. She felt hot tears suddenly pour down her face as she released the long-held grief from her subconscious.

This is one of several processes that can be used to hear your Guides and to validate what you hear. The process is similar to evidential mediumship where the psychic asks for new or unique information to trust the accuracy of the connection as no intuitive is completely accurate.

***

Gwen took a deep breath, called Lance and asked if he wanted to hear an impression of himself in a past life. He said yes, and she summarized as succinctly as she could what had been happening for the previous few days.

There was a long silence at the end of her recounting of what had occurred regarding this shared past life possibility.

Finally, she asked him tentatively, 'What's your first impression?'

He replied slowly, 'I'll have to sit with it. I can't believe I've been anyone as important as William Shakespeare. I admire him greatly, as you know. But I'm not clear if Shakespeare wrote the works himself, or if Sir Francis Bacon or someone else did. The history is unclear.'

Gwen knew there were many questions about the authorship of William Shakespeare's large and important body of work. She nodded her understanding.

Lance told her he would have to feel into it over time. This is a wise course to take with a potential past life, particularly if the impression is shared by someone else vs. learning of it yourself first-hand via a hypnotherapy session or your own meditation, dreams, spontaneous recall or clairvoyant senses.

She told him she respected his approach and agreed with it. If someone had randomly told her out of the blue she'd been Anne Hathaway, let alone William Shakespeare, she likely would have asked them cheekily if their Mom had dropped them on their head as a baby?

***

'Lance, one more thing,' Gwen said quietly. 'Your response is perfectly logical and intelligent, yet very left-brained. What does your GUT say about whether you were Shakespeare? Close your eyes – what was the first thing you felt when I asked you if you could have been Will Shakespeare?'

She heard him take a deep breath, and sensed his vibration rising and connection with his Guides strengthening.

Lance's reply was slow and measured. 'I saw you as Anne Hathaway in the 1500s. I also immediately thought of Anne Hathaway, the actress today.'

Gwen felt tears well up as he validated her past life. She hadn't expected he'd be able to do that. He saw her as Anne Hathaway, but still was not sure if he'd been Will?

She realized that was another possibility. Gwen let that go to follow the other line of inquiry as it felt much stronger.

'Yes, what about the current Anne Hathaway? What's your connection with her – it's more than just being a fan, isn't it? Is there a more personal connection? I sense a connection we're meant to unravel. Is there a deeper meaning why we've gone to so many of her movies together?'

'You're dead on. I met her mother when I was traveling with my football team back in high school. It was an away game – far away. God, we were on that bus for hours! She lived in a different state. The girl who would later become Anne Hathaway's mother was the next-door neighbor to the people I stayed with that weekend.'

Gwen commented quietly, 'That's fascinating. You're doing great. What happened next,' she remarked, without realizing she had begun to use Past-Life Regression phrasing as they were already deep into that energy.

Author and film director Rich Martini describes this now occurring in his everyday life in his thought-provoking book, 'Hacking the Afterlife.'

'One minute you're having coffee with a friend – and the next minute you're on the flipside,' Rich Martini wrote, referring to the other side of the Veil.

Lance continued. 'We were very drawn to one another but couldn't go out as she had a boyfriend at the time. She became an actress, too, and then gave birth to Anne in the early 1980s, I think it was.'

He paused for a long time. She remained quiet, holding the energy for him. Gwen sensed some regret on his part.

'I never forgot her. It felt like a connection was meant to occur.'

It was now Gwen's turn to be silent for a long moment.

'Lance, that's compelling synchronicity. What if you were one of the men meant to marry her mother this lifetime and to become the modern-day actress Anne Hathaway's father? What if you were possibly also Anne Hathway's husband Will in the sixteenth century?'

'Hmmm. Tell me more. You've got more pieces of the puzzle than I do, Gwen. I can almost see your brain all lit up as you put this together in various configurations. Keep shuffling the puzzle pieces – I'm following you."

'We know it's well-documented in the afterlife research that we play different roles with our soul group members in multiple lives. Research also shows there can be more than one person who's meant to play a role – like an understudy in a play,' she replied.

'Yes,' he said simply. 'Go on.'

'What if you had met the current day Anne Hathaway's mother again in some remarkable way if the man who became her husband didn't present, or they didn't get together, or stay together – like an understudy taking over for the lead?'

His reply was straight to the point. 'Yes. Agreed. I see that was likely part of my life path.'

She nodded. 'I see that too. Let's not forget Will Shakespeare was an actor as well as playwright, and the Shakespeare family income was from The Globe Theater, not from his plays being published,' Gwen replied.

'That came later,' she continued rapidly. 'It would not surprise me if today's Anne Hathaway and her mother and possibly more of her family also lived in the time of Shakespeare. It's why they chose that name for her – to help one or more of them remember. They may have energy from that timeline to release or brought their acting abilities forward in time to work with again.'

There was a long pause.

'A rose by any other name would smell as sweet,' Lance remarked thoughtfully.

Gwen got his double entendre immediately. It was both a line from Romeo & Juliet, written by Shakespeare, and Lance was also referring to her last name – Gwendolyn Rose.

'Yes,' she said. 'Keep going.'

'It doesn't matter what someone's name is – though I agree with you that names are often clues to our past lives – or what the person looks like,' he continued.

"It's all about the energy,' Lance concluded. 'Energy never lies, and that's what people need to get really good at reading, just like we both read each other's energy and recognized each other when we met again this lifetime.'

Gwen smiled sweetly as both hung up at the same time. Neither needed to say another word.

***

It would be several years before they would find more evidence of the Will Shakespeare and Anne Hathaway timeline in the tiny town of Othello, Washington.

'Othello' was another Shakespeare play. Lance and Gwen were on a past life pilgrimage to search for clues regarding a different past life as obscure 1800s married writers Gretchen and John Elliott when they found additional clues regarding their past life as William Shakespeare and Anne Hathaway.

Gwen realized one of her favorite quotes was from Hamlet, "There are more things on heaven and earth, Horatio, than are dreamt of in your philosophy."

That quote perfectly expressed her desire to be open-minded in life – discerning yes, yet also flexible and willing to consider new ideas and possibilities based on the best evidence she could find.

***

We return now to my life as Ann Warren in Colonial America, having established an intriguing possibility why I so loved reading William Shakespeare.

I believe I chose an incarnation as Anne Hathaway and married Will in England in the 1500s. I next incarnated as Anna Warren, born in England, and emigrated to what would become New England in the New World.

It feels like a natural progression. First there was Will Shakespeare and Anne Hathaway, and then William Pierce and Ann Warren in my very next life?

***

Having the same first names feels like a thread to pull to connect the two lifetimes. I've noticed souls often choose similar names in some incarnations, or even choose the same first letter for their name repeatedly, as we leave breadcrumbs to pick up at the right time in the future.

The first past life I found was in 2011 during a formal Past-Life Regression with a Michael Newton therapist in Seattle. I was a wealthy young woman named Annabelle, residing with my family in London in my late teens.

Another version of the name Ann – and London, once again.

I later spontaneously found a Sea Captain wife past life as Eliza Ann Webber in Halifax, Nova Scotia. I believe I was again married to Lance's soul that lifetime.

I also found a series of Gwendolyn - Gwen - Wendy - Gwenyth - Guinevere - Gwenafyar - Gwinn incarnations.

***

Was part of why I was so determined as Ann Warren that I was meant to be William Pierce's wife simply leftover energy from our marriage in the previous life?

We'd even both had the same first names. Yes, they are common names, but the same two names in combination is intriguing.

I was also greatly influenced by knowing that William Pierce was my primary soul mate. I heard Spirit tell me that clearly the first time we met aboard ship.

I would be told the same thing by my Guides in 2010. Fortunately, I was able to change that designation as Gwendolyn to open the door to meet a different, much more compatible life partner. I now understood the primary function of a soul mate is to master challenging lessons.

These are fascinating possibilities as we continue to explore the nature of consciousness surviving the death of the physical.

Simon Garfield Bown explores this topic so well with a wide variety of guests on his 'Past Lives Podcast.' Look for his excellent podcast on-line, including on iTunes.

My belief is emotions are timeless, as is energy, wherein the soul remembers everything at some level. We then endure the amnesia wipe to more easily focus on the 'now' moment.

***

It feels appropriate to end this chapter with two favorite Shakespeare quotes:

'All the world's a stage, and all the men and women merely players: they have their exits and their entrances; and one man in his time plays many parts, his acts being seven ages...' *('As You Like It')*

'Shakespeare is the most famous person in the world that no one knows anything about.' *(TNT's 2017 television series 'Will')*

Chapter 6

I resume my narrative as Ann Warren. Two events occurred when I was seventeen that changed the course of not only my life, but my after-life, and my future lives.

Father died suddenly in 1628, five years after our arrival at the Colony. He left behind a grieving wife, five teen daughters and two preschool sons.

1628 was also the year I fell deeply in love with William, but in the wrong lifetime.

I saw Captain William Pierce a handful of times during the first five years after he brought us safely to Plimoth in 1623. It was never enough.

It was energetically a 'Crumbs from the Table' relationship. My Guides told me this repeatedly in both the seventeenth and twenty-first centuries.

I didn't fully learn my lessons with William as Anna Warren, so we played them out again in the years 2010 – 2018. It was much like repeating a grade in school. Not easy at times, but quite necessary and beneficial.

My belief is lessons are offered repeatedly at the soul level until we attain mastery. Instruction typically becomes less subtle in subsequent presentations and is often more dramatic, challenging or downright painful.

My failure to heal and release my experiences with William in a timely manner impacted my soul's journey for over three hundred years. Our relationship was heartbreaking at times as well as a tremendous opportunity to attain increased clarity, skills and wisdom.

I believe the soul craves experiences above all else to have the opportunity to progress. Some experiences are incomprehensible when viewed from the lens of a single human incarnation. They are only understandable when we stand in the light of the full wisdom of our soul.

The purpose of some experiences may remain elusive until we are in a higher vibrational state attained by a spiritual practice such as meditation or past-life regression.

Sometimes they may puzzle us until we work with a spiritual teacher or healer to help interpret them, or even until we are Home with our Guides and/or have our life review.

***

I repeated many aspects of the Plimoth experience with Lance again in the years 2010-12 and to a lesser degree until 2018. I needed to master our multiple souls' contracts which included Lance was to help me 'Wake up spiritually and sexually,' and that he was going to 'Break my heart repeatedly, until I learned to stand in my power fully, without abusing it.'

My belief is we all have multiple romantic soul mates as well as other types of soul mates. No other romantic soul mate except Lance was willing to 'break my heart repeatedly' when we were doing the pre-life planning for my current life.

I'd like to thank him for taking on this challenging and unpopular role with me. Lance was not liked or accepted by my family and many of my friends as a result. They could only see what looked like poor treatment of me on the surface, as they couldn't appreciate our contracts.

But I understood our contracts and the progress we were making at the soul level. Lance did too, as I shared the information with him in detail as transparency was key for us to master our final lessons.

I needed to learn to be my own best friend; to forgive easily; to move on gracefully when a relationship has run its natural course; to stay fully in my power without abusing it; and how to part peacefully when my Guides asked me to, even if I was the only one willing to do so.

I needed to learn to love fearlessly and to give my love fully only to a man who was worthy of it. I needed to 'Love myself first' as a spark of the Divine.

***

My dear friend Abby from Plimoth can best narrate my relationship with William. She is an astute observer and a wise and caring soul I deeply appreciate.

I now turn the narration over to Abby.

I have been Ann's best friend since I arrived at the Colony several years after her. We work side-by-side at the trading post most days.

My family lives next door to the Warrens, one up from the water. The Warren home is closest to the water, the last cottage on the left as you face the harbor.

I keenly feel Ann's great sadness at her father's passing. It has been only a brief fortnight since Richard Warren was taken so suddenly from his family and our small community in the Year of Our Lord 1628.

He contributed much, was a godly, loving family man, and a wonderful neighbor and community Elder.

Richard Warren left behind a large and devastated family. Elizabeth is now a widow in her forties. Ann's eldest sister Mary is nineteen years of age, Ann is seventeen, her younger sisters are fifteen, thirteen and eleven, and those two darling little boys are only aged two and four years.

Mary and Ann are so needed to help Elizabeth hold the family together. Elizabeth looks beyond exhausted and cannot do this on her own.

There is so much death at Plimoth, but there is such a supportive community, great friendships and love here, too.

Ann is trying to stay busy at the trading post today with unneeded vigorous sweeping. I can see she is fighting tears.

My dear friend has lost a shocking amount of weight in the fortnight since her father's death. Her clothes hang loose. She has no color in her face and looks so dispirited.

***

We were flabbergasted when Captain William Pierce suddenly strode into our tiny trading post on that memorable day. Pierce greeted us both cheerily, in his typical breezy, larger-than-life manner, as if we should have expected his arrival all along?

'My dear ladies, I would appreciate your assistance to unload the many fine items I have brought you to help supply the Plantation. It has been a long journey by ship, by shallop, and finally leading this fine specimen of a horse.'

He smiled warmly at both of us as we continued to stare wordlessly at him with surprise.

'Ann, can you be spared from your trading store duties to help unload Arthur with me? He's heavily-laden.'

Captain Pierce looked around pointedly. There was no one in the trading post except Ann and me.

Ann cocked her head at me tiredly, too numb to make this simple decision or even to form words. I urged her to go outside on that beautiful fall day, one which more resembled summer.

'Ann, I can watch over things here, and make room for our new supplies. Why don't you go help Captain Pierce? After all, my last name translates to 'corn for food,' so it seems fitting for me to remain and do any corn trading myself.'

Ann rewarded my attempt at humor with a wan smile. She was so pale and lifeless she more resembled a ghost than a healthy young woman.

My intent was to distract my dear friend from her pressing grief for a few hours. Captain Pierce traveled extensively and would have much news of other parts of the world.

I was aware of Ann's deep yearning for the Captain, many years our senior. I knew of their clandestine relationship, though we never discussed it directly. Some things you just *knew*.

Ann would want to talk with Captain Pierce about her father's sudden passing. I hoped she would somehow find a way to begin to express some of the deep grief in a way she hadn't been able to do with family and friends as we were grieving Richard Warren's loss so deeply, too.

Ann was clearly still taken aback to see Ship's Master Pierce, particularly as he usually arrived in the afternoon. He had never come to our trading locale so early in the morning.

'Yes, I'm happy to help you, Captain Pierce,' Ann finally replied quietly. She looked at me uncertainly again.

I smiled at her. 'Go,' I said gently. 'Enjoy the gift of the beauty of this day and enjoy seeing the new goods we will trade. Go talk with our *great friend* Captain Pierce.'

Highlighting the words 'great friend' was my subtle warning to Pierce. Would he heed them was a crucial concern?

Ann was incredibly vulnerable. I would have to watch him – watch them – closely.

I didn't fully comprehend at that time there was nothing I could do to save Ann from her chosen path. She was choosing to endure deep heartbreak for hundreds of years.

It helps to take a long view of these things. I would help her heal and complete her lesson in a future life, if need be.

I was often Ann's mother or best friend. We are in the same primary soul group and travel together frequently.

But she also has profound history with the soul known both as Captain William Pierce and as her former lover Lance in her current life.

Some of it has not been easy. It's important we learn to have no regrets, and to seize the present moment with as much might as we can muster.

***

Ann and Ship's Master Pierce stepped just outside our miniscule trading post. I could still see and hear them through the single open window and doorway.

'We weren't expecting you, William,' I heard Ann exclaim. 'You've never come in the morning before? But I'm so incredibly happy you're here!'

I overheard Captain Pierce explain a bit loudly what had transpired.

'I had trouble arranging Arthur as there are so few horses here at the Plantation. And you know I strongly prefer to get Arthur – I just love that big white horse! It's like he's a part of me somehow. We need to bring more horses over from England, or ideally more successfully breed them here at the Colony.'

Captain Pierce dropped his voice to continue more gently.

'I arrived yesterday, Ann, but chose to stay overnight to see you. I heard your father passed, and I didn't want to leave without visiting to pay my respects. I'm truly sorry for your incredible loss. I know you must be heartsick. Your father was a brave, hard-working man of great integrity, and one who has done much for the Colony.'

I sensed Ann was working too hard to hold it together to reply.

Pierce continued after a pause as she didn't comment.

'I hear your Father was recognized during his funeral service for being – quote – 'a useful instrument and bearing a deep share of the difficulties and troubles of the first settling of the Plantation of New Plimoth.'

'Is that what was said at his service?' our Ship's Master queried.

'Yes,' Ann returned quietly, amazed and gratified he was quoting verbatim from her father's funeral service, which he had not attended.

'That's exactly right, William.'

I tensed at Ann's use of his first name when they were alone. This was too familiar in our time, especially given our age as compared to Captain Pierce's, as well as his stature in the community.

I knew the Captain must have encouraged Ann more than once to use his first name. But why?

'Where is your father buried? And what age was the good man?' our Ship's Master continued.

'He is buried on Burial Hill, just to the south. Father is – I mean Father was – aged forty-eight years,' Ann replied.

I could hear her voice beginning to break.

I saw Pierce suddenly hug Ann closely. I stiffened with horror. This was not proper in Colonial America, even if he only meant to convey his compassion.

He held her too long and much too closely. She wasn't resisting. My warning bells were clanging loudly.

Was I meant to say something? I was fifteen years of age.

Ann was seventeen, certainly of marriageable age, and not a child. The Captain was in his thirties and a well-educated, worldly man. He knew better than this!

To my great relief he finally released her, just before I stepped outside to interrupt their embrace.

'I'll make every effort to visit your father's grave site and pay my final respects before I leave the Colony,' Pierce said.

Ann smiled happily for the first time I had seen since her father's death.

'Thank you, William,' she said quietly. 'That would mean the world to me.'

I knew Ann took great comfort from Captain Pierce's presence. But what would happen to her fragile state of mind when William Pierce departed, as he inevitably did?

I sensed my dear friend was unintentionally playing with fire. She was going to get burned. The only question was to what degree?

It took them almost an hour to fully unload the handsome, tall white horse named Arthur. Arthur had been named to honor the legendary King Arthur of Camelot.

***

Gwen had a vivid dream in 2013 that Arthur, the horse at Plimoth, had the same soul as William's horse from when William was King Arthur at Camelot.

No wonder Captain Pierce preferred that one horse so strongly. Arthur was potentially his own War Horse from a thousand years earlier and bore his own name from that lifetime.

***

Captain Pierce and Ann efficiently carried the supplies into the trading post. We quickly worked out the trades for these much-needed goods, which were primarily from England.

Most of the items would be traded to our fellow Colonists. A few items I knew we could trade with the Indians who had developed a taste for certain of our English and other European goods.

Captain Pierce informed us he had an almost empty ship to fill to return to England. Therefore, he could accept our beaver furs and bushels of corn in trade as was the custom now that we were in the New World.

The Warrens brought currency over from England and secured it in their home. We seldom used it at the trading post, so did not keep any here.

But the Warrens having Old World legal tender helped make them the natural choice to set up the trading post when the Governor and Elders saw one would be to the Colony's advantage.

Captain Pierce trading for our goods saved us having to procure funds from the Warrens' home. In hindsight, I wondered if Captain Pierce was avoiding Ann's family – Elizabeth in particular – by telling us too quickly we didn't need to obtain currency.

He told us heartily he would 'make us a jolly good trade for our corn and beaver skins!'

I recalled that moment keenly when Ann told me later she had been waiting for him to ask her parents' permission – now only Elizabeth remained – to ask for her hand in marriage.

***

We used little currency at the trading post or in daily life. English currency was essentially useless to the Wampanoag and other tribes as they couldn't trade it easily enough. This greatly devalued our paper and coin currency.

With the Natives, we normally traded our surplus maize for furs, primarily beaver. We then traded the furs as well as surplus corn with Sea Captains for European goods.

Most of the wealth in our time was being accumulated in possessions such as furnishings and clothing, or in land and livestock. The Natives had acquired a taste for our English fine wares and furnishings which made these items even more valuable.

Wampum, the beautiful, precisely strung and counted beads had revolutionized trading a year earlier. Wampum was introduced to the Colony by a visitor from the New Netherlands.

Wampum took up little space, unlike bushels of corn and furs, did not go bad, and was highly valued by the Indians. But wampum was so new we didn't have much of it yet, and Captain Pierce would have no use for it even if we did.

So, we traded goods on the surface. And somehow, we also traded away too much of Ann's heart. She didn't yet understand 'Dog Medicine' – to be her own best friend.

***

Dog medicine wouldn't be fully mastered until she would become involved with dog rescue work beginning in 2016. Volunteering with the Dog Gone Seattle Rescue would teach Gwen to ground her energy and to fully be in the present moment, the 'now' moment, among many other valuable lessons.

***

I noted with silent concern – disapproval, more accurately – that Captain Pierce had a gift for Ann, as always. It was not proper for him to be giving her gifts, nor should she have accepted them.

Gifts carry a palpable energy and can become a tie that binds as they're an energetic exchange.

Usually the gift was a book. I remember once it was the highly coveted and quite valuable William Shakespeare's First Folio.

Ann overly treasured these gifts from Captain Pierce. She would have been wise to gently turn them down, or if that was not possible, to quietly give them to another.

Ann read too much into the Captain's gifts to her. My dear friend was a woman of high integrity and honest to a fault, but I knew she didn't tell her family the full truth regarding where these gifts originated.

Ann would simply say, 'I traded for it at the trading post,' if one of her parents or sisters gently questioned the source of her rare new possession?

I don't think she fully understood what she was 'trading' for these trinkets from him. Ann was giving Captain Pierce too much of her immense love.

Ann didn't understand her love for William Pierce and her devotion to him wasn't valued in the way she needed and deserved, though he did care for her in his own selfish way.

His caring for her only made it worse, from what I was able to observe. Much worse, just like it would when they would meet again in 2010.

William had Ann hooked like a helpless fish on a lne. But it was a line that he was neither reeling in nor releasing.

Ann was giving away her power by allowing herself to be hooked by him. I was deeply concerned how this would end for my best friend in 1628.

*****

I became concerned over time when Gwen and Lance reunited on Match.com in 2010 – oh, the irony – and resumed an unusual romance that would almost destroy her. He again kept her neatly sequestered from his friends and family, which was a red flag she recognized, but didn't know how to resolve.

Yet I knew she had to move forward with him to clean up the old energy from our shared Colonial America past. At first, I encouraged her to move forward with him.

Over time, I could do nothing more than simply be there for her. She'd make her own choices.

Both times she chose heartbreak.

It took Gwen's soul more than three hundred years to heal her heartbreak from the 1600s. Thankfully, she finally unhooked herself from the old snare by moving into her power after an intense on-again/ off-again romance spanning several years.

But this time William's soul gave her the great gift of closure that she had so desperately needed when he ended their romance in 2011. This was the hand-up she had very much needed and showed significant growth on Lance's part as it wasn't easy to do.

***

Back in 1628, Captain Pierce cheerfully told Ann as they re-entered the post, 'I'm so hungry I could eat a bear! I haven't eaten yet today and saw precious little for tea-time or my supper last eve. You *must*, Ann, you simply *must* break bread with me, especially as our friend Abby already dined on her own.'

He was correct – I had just finished eating my modest lunch at the trading post counter. I was carefully re-folding the paper I'd wrapped my small meal in to re-use again on the morrow.

I was gratified to hear Ann laugh for the first time in weeks. I knew she was amused because this was trademark William, and that Lance – his Future Self – had said that same thing to Gwen almost every day she saw him.

She told me she never understood how such a tall, strong man could eat so little food – perhaps it was due to his many years at sea?

Both Ann and I had experienced the unappetizing food during our one long voyage. We knew first-hand how food and drink could become so limited in quantity, as well as variety, especially if men were at sea longer than expected.

Captain Pierce continued a tad forcefully in this vein.

'Ann, I have some tasty food with me in Arthur's saddlebag. I know a beautiful place where we can eat our lunch. Can you be spared from the trading post? It seems exceptionally quiet here. Abby, can you handle this on your own for a while for our dear Ann's sake?'

He turned to look at me expectantly, exerting the full force of his formidable personality and will.

Ann was studying me carefully. I felt something critical hang in the balance.

I knew the Captain would pull rank, use his considerable charm, negotiate powerfully, cajole, argue, or even pout until I capitulated. Pierce seemed to *always* get his way.

This concerned me greatly. I felt something was at a critical juncture, though I could not have said exactly what.

I took a deep breath and made my decision. I encouraged Ann to have lunch with him as it was so lovely outside, thinking they would be in full view of anyone passing by. Nothing unseemly would be possible.

'Ann, the Captain is quite right. The post is remarkably quiet today. I will keep busy organizing these wonderful supplies our friend – I again stressed the word 'friend' as hard as I could – Captain Pierce has brought us. Just take your lunch with you and go. I'll get things *ship-shape* here and await your return to close up together.'

Both Ann and William laughed heartily at my simple pun – they so often laughed at the same things and were so animated in their conversations together. There was a deep friendship and remarkable connection between them that was not well-known in the Colony. They seemed to almost read each other's minds.

***

That energy immediately rekindled when they began dating in 2010. I again was the observer as they joyfully, animatedly finished each other's sentences, beginning on their first date.

I had never heard Gwen so excited and happy as when she called me immediately after meeting Lance. She was higher than a kite. It sounded like he was intrigued, too, or why would such a busy man have stayed for a three-hour lunch on a weekday?

But the reality was they certainly weren't meeting for the first time. None of us were.

Lance could still read Gwen's most subtle body language or facial expressions like a book, whereas few could as she was skilled in controlling her presentation.

She could still powerfully connect to him telepathically with little effort, as could he to her, especially in the dream time.

I again was gravely concerned. This time she had to finish it – on her terms – or I knew they would meet again. Or she would meet someone else to help her complete this elusive set of lessons.

Lance also had much to learn from Gwen. I sensed they were teaching soul mates for one another.

***

Ann gathered her lunch and thanked me. There was finally some color back in her pale face as she and Captain Pierce left the trading post. I could see how her eyes had brightened. They suddenly looked too bright as she was nothing but raw nerves and a sea of emotions.

After that they were out of my purview. Ann now resumes her own narration.

***

I looked up at William expectantly once we were outside, wondering where he planned for us to walk to eat our mid-day meal?

We were alone for the moment on that picture-perfect, early autumn day. To my great shock, he gave me a quite improper lingering hug and a kiss full on the lips! William then grabbed me around my waist before I could protest and lifted me up onto Arthur.

Arthur was clearly William's favorite horse of the few we had in the Colony. William personally brought Arthur over from England, which was not easy to do in our time period.

William must be planning to lead the horse with me on it, I realized, like he had lead Arthur in with the supplies. I smiled happily. What a rare treat this would be.

William again surprised me.

'Ann, move forward in the saddle as far as you can,' Pierce commanded, in a take-no-prisoners tone.

'Pull your skirts tight behind you to make enough room.'

He led Arthur over to a stump and climbed up behind me onto the horse. I was stunned. I knew we shouldn't be riding together in this familiar way.

Our bodies were squeezed together in the single saddle. I could feel *all* of William pressed into the back of my body, through my thin golden-yellow cotton blouse and matching skirt.

What if someone saw us? My reputation would be tarnished or even ruined. I would bring shame on my family, who was already suffering so much from Father's sudden death.

Before I could remind William sharply that this wasn't proper, it wasn't proper at all, he brought the reins around me, around us. He steered Arthur briskly toward the woods.

I made the critical decision to just be quiet and enjoy this incredible moment, which would likely never come again. We were unlikely to be seen in the woods.

Riding horseback was a rare treat, and with this man I so loved, of all men on Earth?

I finally admitted to myself I loved William with all my heart. I wanted nothing more than to spend my life with him. I was in seventh heaven!

I would accept the risk to my reputation William was creating as we were not yet formally courting, but I felt certain soon would be.

***

A half hour later, we had fallen into a companionable silence. We had caught up quickly on the highlights of our lives since we had last seen one another.

William spoke of his adventures at sea and his time in foreign ports and lands. He of course had news of England, which I quite relished.

I hung on his every word. I was bewitched by William. I never noted his omission about his time spent at his own home down south in the Virginia Colony.

***

Arthur continued to pick his way sure-footedly along a narrow trail through the woods. I could now hear running water. I sensed there might be a small clearing up ahead as it seemed brighter.

William pulled up on the reins to give Arthur a well-deserved rest. He dismounted and reached up wordlessly to lift me down. I went into his arms more and more easily, gazing at him with adoration.

William allowed our horse to drink from the stream in large, satisfied gulps. He gathered some of the clear moving water in a small cup from his saddlebag. William drank from it after ensuring I had my fill first from the same cup.

Sharing a cup stirred memories of an earlier life together. Once again, I heard 'Camelot!'

My Guides continued, 'You need to remember your time together as King and Queen of Camelot to heal it. You both need to master forgiveness.'

When our Future Selves shared wine from the same glass starting in 2010, I would feel the present time slip away and would travel back to Camelot.

***

I shook my head gently to clear it. I wanted to just delight in the present moment. I'd work through my memories of Camelot – also known as Avalon – later.

Several large branches were missing from where there had been a lightning strike years ago. It allowed the dappled sunshine to peek through.

It truly was a lovely spot that had caught William's eye on his way to the trading post early that morning. We sat on a fallen cedar log that formed a natural bench.

We traded food from our meal rations as I had a small bag of foodstuffs, too, expecting to be at the post for the day.

When we had finished our meal and had more water from the stream, William looked at me expectantly. My eyes danced with delight and told him yes.

He hugged and kissed me again thoroughly. We had never had this much privacy or time alone together. My heart was suddenly bursting with joy.

***

The irony was we were *not* alone. Several native men had been out hunting or quietly going about their business when we noisily blundered into the clearing, talking aloud to one another as we rode together on that blazingly white horse.

Several men were observing our tryst.

I felt my heart beating so rapidly with immense love and desire. I knew I had loved William with all my heart since I had first recognized him as my primary soul mate five years earlier aboard ship.

Perhaps 'Love at First Sight' implies a previous shared lifetime or soul contract?

My mind skipped ahead feverishly. William would need to ask Elizabeth for my hand in marriage now that Father was gone.

Would Elizabeth grant it, knowing how much older William was than me? I was seventeen, and he was in his early thirties. I didn't care a whit!

More importantly, where would I live – would I travel with him on board his ships, a dangerous and uncomfortable life at best? But we would be together, so of course this was my strong preference.

***

Gwen would later remember a life married to Lance, again a Sea Captain. They had a large family together in Halifax, Nova Scotia, and she had memories of being involved with the Underground Railroad.

Was my desire in 1628 somehow so strong it came true two hundred years later in Canada? Our thoughts do create our reality, as explained eloquently by Penney Peirce in 'Frequency: The Power of Personal Vibration.'

***

Would I marry William but remain behind with my family? Or would he move me down to his home in Jamestowne? Or would I return to his home in England?

Could I be spared from helping my family now that Father was gone, I mused. I was one of the two oldest, along with Mary.

Elizabeth had too much to do with three younger girls, plus two young sons. And we had to support our large family of eight in the New World without Father, which would not be easy.

What was the right thing for me to do? Would I be allowed to follow my heart? Where did my duty lie?

What about my tremendous love for William? I couldn't imagine my life without him.

I came out of my brown study with a start when William said, 'Kiss me again, Ann, before I take you back. You are wonderful company, as always. I need to get you back now, and to take care of some things before I head out to the ship. I want to have time to visit your father's grave.'

Ship? Father's grave?

He was leaving again, I realized with a sinking heart. He was leaving, always leaving…

But first William will surely talk with Elizabeth when he brings me back to the trading post, I thought contentedly. Our home is so close by. William will ask to speak with Elizabeth, and we will go find her together.

A few of the Native men shook their heads sadly, somehow knowing this would not end well for the young Colonial girl they recognized from the post.

They may not have understood every word we spoke but could easily read the body language of a young woman who was madly in love with an older man. And that he had a ship in every port.

***

Those few hours with William were some of the happiest hours of the first seventeen years of my life, despite my deep sadness over Father's sudden leaving.

We arrived back at the trading post too soon for my liking. William dismounted easily, jumping down agilely onto the same stump.

He was almost feline in his movements at times as William was so well-coordinated and graceful, yet there was nothing feminine about him. He remained masculine in the extreme.

William reached up to help me down. I stretched my arms toward him eagerly. He pretended to be clumsy and set me practically atop him.

I shrieked with delight, sounding a little shrill as I was so happy and nervous both. This was the big moment I'd been living for!

We were standing with the tall horse between us and the trading post where Abby would be closing things up for the day. William looked around quickly to make sure no one was within sight.

He hugged and kissed me deeply one more time before immediately remounting Arthur rather than tying him to the post as I expected.

'I'll be back for you, Ann,' he said quietly, with a beaming smile and cheery wave.

'I'll be back when you're just a little older.'

He began to ride Arthur briskly away before I could ask timidly didn't he want to speak with Elizabeth?

I dug deep to manufacture my cheeriest smile and waved in return as he turned toward me a final time.

The last thing he said to me was, 'Wait for me, Ann. Always know you are so incredibly special to me, and the very best company!'

***

I would still be waiting for William at some level upon my death in 1676, almost fifty years later.

William had said he would be back for me. In my world, promises were kept.

I felt crushed William hadn't arranged to talk with Elizabeth to ask for my hand in marriage and for her permission to begin formally courting.

Was it too soon after Father's death? Or perhaps William was waiting for my eighteenth birthday?

I simply knew he would ask for my hand the next time we were together. I would have to be patient, once again, as I never knew when he would arrive back to the New Colony.

I would climb the big rock whenever I could to watch for William. I would wait for him to break through the woods leading Arthur or I would dig clams down by the water to surreptitiously watch for his ship.

I couldn't wait for us to be formally courting – I could see clearly that marriage was our destiny. I couldn't stop smiling as I dreamily floated into the trading post.

Abby took one look at my face and knew my fate was sealed. I had fully given my heart to Captain William Pierce. I had given him not just all my love, but my actual heart.

***

I never considered William would not return for me.

My heart broke completely from Pierce's crushing, puzzling absence after what I took to be his promise we would be together as man and wife. I was also deeply wounded by the lack of closure and difficult timing in combination with Father's death.

I waited for my love William, for my Sea Captain and primary soul mate for five long years. I climbed the big rock repeatedly to peer through the woods, visualizing that tall, well-built man breaking into the clearing leading a heavily-laden Arthur.

I would see his face light up with joy when he saw me! If we had privacy, he would open his arms wide, and I would clamber down the rock and run to him. Our long separation would be gone in an instant.

Instead, I never saw William Pierce again.

Gwen would later replace her own heart chakra in 2017 with the help of a Shaman as she had not been able to heal her heart since that experience.

Chapter 7

Gwendolyn Rose was blessed as a newlywed to purchase a home in picturesque Boxford, Massachusetts with her husband Jake.

There were many nights when Gwen would clairvoyantly see a girl from an earlier time repeatedly climb a large rock on their rustic two-acre property.

The young woman was dressed in Colonial-era clothing. She wore a bright yellow-gold skirt and matching long-sleeved blouse with a white apron and matching white kerchief on her head.

The girl was always peering anxiously toward the woods, facing East toward the water. Gwen sensed she was longing for her love to return.

Occasionally Gwen would see a tall, handsome man break through the woods, leading a heavily laden tall white horse. He would begin to approach the girl.

Maddeningly, he would always fade away before arriving at the young woman's side, providing no relief, no closure.

Their coming together felt like an elusive orgasm that just couldn't be reached. It was such incredibly frustrating energy, rather like an open circuit or endless loop.

***

Gwen didn't fully grasp what was occurring at the time she lived in Boxford in the late 1980s and early 1990s. She was located sixty-five miles north of Plymouth, Massachusetts.

Gwen didn't understand at the time she was directly involved in this centuries-old drama. She thought she was simply an observer because the girl had lived on the same property long ago.

This powerful unresolved energy loop continued for more than three hundred years. The image of the yearning girl waiting and watching from the rock for her love appeared to Gwen many times during the four years she and Jake lived in their large Colonial home.

It would take twenty more years, a cross-country move and a reunion with the man who had been Captain William Pierce to understand she was seeing her own ghost – her own Earth-bound energy – from an earlier lifetime.

***

Ann Warren's presence was so strong in the years Gwen and Jake lived in the house that three overnight guests sensed Ann's ghost, too.

Yet Gwen had never mentioned her strange experiences seeing the young girl climb the rock and wait with great anticipation for her love to appear as she didn't know what to make of the visions.

Jake didn't want to discuss it, and she knew her mother wouldn't either, so she kept the strange happenings to herself for years.

Gwen had simply asked her guests how they slept after their first night in her home. She wanted to know if they needed more blankets or bath towels to be comfortable while visiting, like any good hostess would.

Gwen was stunned when three different visitors reported strange vivid dreams about a brokenhearted young girl from long ago. Each shared with her a bit hesitantly during their separate visits that the girl kept climbing up a large rock and peering through the woods in the direction of the water, located to the East.

How could some of Gwen's guests have the same dream she had so many times without her ever mentioning it?

This was surreal and an unprecedented mystery.

***

Gwen didn't understand Mass Consciousness or the Collective Unconscious at the time. None of them understood her friends were trying to help her remember and validate her own past life so she could heal and release old energy that no longer served her.

Her friends were equally mystified as they had no experience in this arena either, and none of them knew who to discuss this odd occurrence with. This was also before the days of easy Internet searching.

Yet all of them felt strongly the heartbroken young girl was endlessly waiting for her beloved to return. It felt like a cruel time-warp parody of the Old Spice television commercial where the woman was always waiting for "Her Man to Come Home from the Sea."

But he never came. And her soul didn't know how to stop waiting. She was horrifically stuck, like an animal caught in a punishing trap that didn't quite have the courage or strength to gnaw off its own limb and escape.

***

Gwen returned to her former Boxford property about a year after she sent Ann Warren Little's ghost Home to the Light. Jake and Gwen had sold the home and moved to Seattle more than two decades earlier.

She was relieved there was no sign of either Ann or the rock she'd climbed so endlessly, rather like Sisyphus in his eternal punishment rolling a heavy boulder to the top of a mountain only to have it roll down again, for eternity.

Gwen was flabbergasted to a moment later clairvoyantly see Captain William Pierce break through the woods leading Arthur, his big white horse.

The Ship's Master hesitated when he saw her. She sensed he was confused to see her standing quietly in the cul-de-sac next to her rental car as she looked like she does now, and he would never have seen an automobile as he had lived in the 1600s.

Yet Gwen knew he recognized her at some level as Ann. He seemed a bit conflicted to see her.

Gwen took a deep breath to raise her vibration and ask her Guides why, as she sensed the Plimoth energy was healed.

***

She immediately heard 'King Arthur.' Gwendolyn – formerly Guinevere – asked William's soul for his forgiveness for when she broke his heart at Camelot cuckolding him with his best friend Lancelot.

Gwen was relieved when he nodded solemnly in response to her request could he please find it in in his heart to forgive her?

She bowed her head to him in repentance and noticed her hands had arranged themselves over her heart.

He continued to gaze at her expectantly, without saying a word. Gwen realized he needed her forgiveness in return.

She took a deep breath. As she blew it out slowly, she forgave him both for Camelot and for breaking her heart at Plimoth.

He continued to look at her patiently at first, head cocked to the right, eventually crossing his arms and tapping his foot to convey he'd need to leave soon.

She took another deep breath and told him she forgave him for the heartbreak she'd felt with him in their current life and for any other lifetime together.

He smiled faintly and moved his right hand quickly in circles, signaling to her to keep going.

She asked for his forgiveness, through all space and time and in any life form or dimension.

Might as well be thorough about this, Gwen thought ruefully. The scope of this lesson has been unprecedented.

She heaved a sigh of relief as she felt so many ghosts – at least one of them literal – laid to rest between them.

William tipped his hat to her, turned Arthur around smartly, and walked back toward the woods at the edge of her former property. He faded away the moment he was within the tree line, though she could see some sparkles of light for a moment, especially from the horse. Gwen now saw Arthur in his higher vibrational form as a unicorn.

She breathed a deep sigh of relief and started to get into her rental car. Gwen was sweating on the hot summer day and ready to turn on the air conditioning.

But she heard 'Wait – you have one more thing to make right.'

**

Gwen stood for another moment and stilled her mind. She asked her wise, supportive Guides for insight.

Gwen suddenly realized that Jake – now her former husband – had lived with her in this house, and that he was also her spurned suitor from Plimoth.

Ouch! What if he was still mired in old emotions and stuck energies with her, too, though she'd tried to be kind and respectful with him and to cut the cords?

Did she need to make something right with Jake, though they'd been divorced for a decade? Yes – that was it. He was not happy she had rejected him at Plimoth as she was pining for Pierce and then married Thomas Little.

And now here she was at their former home from when they were newlyweds, interacting with Pierce once again, who she had met and dated years after her divorce from Jake. It was an energetic open wound for him.

She repeated the ritual of asking Jake for his forgiveness across all space and time and dimensions, past, present and future.

Gwen waited until she heard a slightly grudging, 'Yes. It's done. Let's move on.'

She thanked him and offered Jake her forgiveness easily, as she now knew it was the path to her freedom!

Gwen heaved a sigh of relief and got into her rental car quickly. She was relieved no one had interrupted her or called the police to check on the odd sight of an unknown woman standing so long in the street peering intently into the yard and woods around a home that she no longer owned.

Gwen didn't understand when she had asked her Guides to provide privacy to do this important work, they had raised her vibration and that of the car to the point they were no longer visible to the human eye. Her Guides then ensured no one stumbled or drove into them.

***

Back at Plimoth, Abby kept Ann's secret of her heartbreaking love for William for the remainder of their lives. The romantic and naïve Ann couldn't seem to let it go as there had been no closure, and she knew William was her primary soul mate.

Didn't being primary soul mates indicate their destiny was to be happy together? Ann didn't understand the primary purpose for soul mates is to provide us with lessons. Many lessons are not easy, though all are worthwhile as our souls can then progress.

***

Neither Abby nor Gwen remembered their lifetime together at Plimoth until both woke up spiritually.

That awakening, in combination with Gwen reuniting with the soul she recognized as Captain William Pierce as well as King Arthur and Will Shakespeare was enough to fully open the floodgates of the Akashic Records of all her lives in a most extraordinary way.

With these profound memories came the opportunity to fully heal. This allowed her to then move into her life purpose and larger soul mission work.

Gwen's healing was extremely challenging until she learned how to clear and balance her own energy daily, how to ground it, and how to raise her vibration and frequency.

***

Ann's eldest sister Mary was the only person beside Abby who knew of Ann's hopeless love for William. Mary became quite frustrated with her romantic younger sister as the years went on.

The ever-practical Mary didn't understand why Ann had so much trouble moving on from William, who was clearly not going to return or to marry her sister! Case closed.

Mary became a second parent to her six younger siblings to help fill the gap after Richard's death, especially as Ann was young for her age. Mary and Elizabeth became even closer after Richard's death as they had to provide for, protect, and lead the large family in the uncertain times of the New World.

***

Mary incarnated in 1998 as Gwen's youngest daughter.

Gwen could sense a strong 'I know better than you about this relationship, and it isn't going to end well' feeling from Tanya from the start once Gwen met Lance – the former Captain William Pierce – in 2010.

Her daughter was only twelve at the time, yet she was also a highly experienced soul who had incarnated many times, including having prepared Earth for its first human inhabitants.

At some level she remembered Pierce's poor treatment of her younger sister, now her mother.

The old Plimoth Plantation energy was even more convoluted in Gwen's current life because Tanya's father in present day was her mother's 'spurned suitor' from Plimoth.

During the 1600s Tanya's mother Gwen – previously her younger sister – had loved William Pierce, rejected John Totman's courtship, and a few years later married Thomas Little.

The unresolved energy was so strong it carried forward in time to provide another opportunity to clear it. Gwen didn't understand at first that emotions are timeless and may need to be healed and released for a soul to become energetically 'unstuck' to progress once again.

***

Lance told Gwen in September of 2011 that one of the main reasons he chose to end their romance was because 'Your family is never going to accept me. And family is very important to both of us.'

He was right. It didn't make her any less heartbroken.

She'd have to slog her way through not one, but two Dark Nights of the Soul and many other challenging experiences to finally embody the 5D – the fifth spiritual dimension – 'Heaven on Earth' energies of peace, love and joy.

***

Ann now resumes her life's story at new Plimoth.

We healed the best we could from Father's death. Father and Elizabeth hadn't had enough time together – only eight or nine years.

Their marriage included three years' separation with Elizabeth back in England with us, while Father was in the New World. They also had seven children to raise, care for and support.

Life at the Plantation continued to be challenging. We continued to exist largely on what we could provide for ourselves. We also had to repay our debts to the Dorchester Company, the financiers for Plimoth Plantation.

The irony that we were working so incredibly hard to pay off William's older brother, the same William who had played me for a fool with his broken promises was not lost on me.

I was heartbroken. I was angry! I felt abandoned. And I needed to keep my relationship with William a secret to preserve my reputation, and my family's good name.

***

It was now three years after Father's death and William's painful, puzzling disappearance. Where had my love gone? Did he never love me? Or was he simply incredibly selfish and unaware of the ramifications of his actions?

I replayed every moment I'd spent with William much too often in my mind. After meeting – reuniting, more accurately – with him aboard the Anne of London in 1623, I saw him again in 1624 at the New Colony when he was Ship's Master for the Charity.

Captain Pierce brought us our first cattle from England that year. He returned as Captain of the Jacob in 1625. If memory serves, that was the year he brought Arthur and a few other precious horses over for us.

I can't recall how many visits there were during 1626 and 1627. I do know he found me privately each time, typically at the trading post.

I saw him more often than once a year as my memory from my time at Plimoth tends to work in seasons, as that was the rhythm of our life as growers.

William always brought me a small discreet gift such as a book, fabric, specialty foods or flowers. Something I would treasure as I couldn't easily obtain it for myself and because it was from him, but that wouldn't be noticeable.

My favorite gifts of all were Shakespeare's First Folio, which I kept for my entire lifetime, and the red roses. I dried them carefully and saved them for years.

***

1628 stands out clearly in my memory due to my father's death and it being the last time I saw William.

I learned much later that Captain Pierce returned with the Mayflower in 1629 and the Lyon in 1630, 1631, and 1632. It was a blessing in disguise he no longer came to see me at the trading post. I see now he sent a Ship's Officer in his place to complete the necessary trades.

I finally moved on from waiting for William to return. That was exceptionally hard to do due to the depth of my love for him, amplified by our many lifetimes together, and the ambiguous way our relationship ended.

***

It's why Gwen sought closure with Lance so hard when he ended their romance in September of 2011 (9/11 – 911, the universal distress signal) after telling her repeatedly, 'We're good!' when they tried to work through the challenges in their relationship.

Sadly, they were NOT good, though both had tried with everything they had as both so wanted their romance to succeed.

This created such an energy dent in Gwen's aura that a gifted energetic chiropractor picked up on it several years later. Dr. Nels Rasmussen helped her heal the imprint using the BEST (Bio-Energetic Synchronization Technique) healing process.

Gwen needed to heal her ability to trust, as it was a cumulative challenge from many lifetimes. This would take her several years to accomplish.

Lance and Gwen greatly needed to resolve the old lower vibration energy binding them together in the form of karmic cords, also known as attachments.

I am so incredibly happy as well as relieved that has finally been accomplished at the soul level with help Gwen received from gifted healers, a few patient friends, and the love of her mystified current day family.

Her family understandably couldn't begin to appreciate what was occurring for her with Lance – it took her years to sort it out herself.

***

I wouldn't learn until hundreds of years later that William's second wife Jane gave birth to their third child in 1633.

I never knew as Ann he was married and had children! What a stunning oversight.

***

I met Jane's Future Self at a large business luncheon as Gwen. I sensed from the second Jane saw me she was petrified of me at our one and only meeting.

I don't normally get this reaction from people.

Jane – who once again had the same name - had to shake my hand as a business convention. Her hand was literally shaking in mine, and I could feel the old Colonial America energy between us.

I have since meditated to apologize to Jane's Higher Self as I have no idea how to find her in the physical, or what I would say. It is never too late to apologize.

Her Higher Self graciously accepted my apology immediately, and both our vibrations moved up.

***

Why did William never tell me the truth? We could have simply been friends. Why didn't someone tell me he was not available that lifetime? No one spoke to me discreetly.

Perhaps few at the Plantation knew of his wife or children or would dream that a young Colonial girl would be romantically interested in a man many years her senior, especially a man who was always at sea.

Arguably he merrily played me for a fool, feeding his own large, yet fragile ego. Yet I need to own my part as possibly the most stubborn, naive woman on the planet.

***

The pure heartbreak of my tone when I finally realized during Gwen's 2013 hypnotherapy session that William was never available is stunning.

The raw emotion in my cry of 'OH, NO!' when I put the pieces together that he was always married would make anyone think twice about being a heartbreaker.

It was not easy to learn I had been a heartbreaker myself, though I'd always suspected it as a happy, healthy romance has been so elusive for me this lifetime.

I was a female heartbreaker several times and a male Don Juan in another life. I needed this painful lesson with Lance to balance my own heartbreaker karmic scales for having been thoughtless or unkind with other people's tender hearts.

When we don't learn our soul-level lessons, we're given another opportunity to do so until we master the learning. A repeated lesson is often more dramatic and painful as we didn't complete it in the subtler form.

Clearly, I needed to take responsibility for my failings which I was not capable of at the time. I was as stubborn as an ox that this relationship was meant to work, despite the obvious reality, and certainly didn't know how to move on graciously or to forgive him either in Colonial America or in my current life. We kept unexpectedly meeting again so I could get it right.

Life is immensely challenging when you love another at the soul level but cannot reconcile core values. When a man (or a woman) loves you, but isn't 'in love' with you, it's a recipe for disaster.

Move on graciously and love yourself first was the lesson it took me several hundred years to master.

***

I would learn centuries later that William was living large in Virginia while I was pining for him as Ann Warren.

The William Pierces had seventeen hundred planted acres and more than thirty servants. William was a powerful, respected and accomplished man in our day.

But William's wife Jane died, as had his first wife whom he married when he was only twenty years of age. I suspect his parents were trying to settle him down with that first early marriage, or perhaps a child was on the way.

William remarried a third time rather than taking the opportunity to pursue his relationship with me – his promise to return when I was older was unfulfilled, creating such a painful, open energetic loop.

***

I didn't know about William's marriages and children until 2013 when I had my first Quantum Healing Hypnotherapy session as Gwen.

We had so much to resolve when we re-met in 2010, yet much of what occurred was amazing! I have no regrets, as the ride was so worth the fall, and needed to happen for me to progress.

It took me years to learn to be peaceful with Lance after our breakup. These were primarily my issues to resolve. The healing and releasing came in stages, as is often the case.

First, I resolved our karmic relationship with his kind assistance and full participation. That was extremely challenging, but necessary for the ghost of Ann Warren Little to be willing to finally travel to the Light.

Later that week I had our primary soul mate designation removed. This was surprisingly hard on my heart. I kept with it doggedly, though, as I was finally learning to be my own best friend – the Native American 'dog medicine' I mentioned earlier.

I realized when I saw him unexpectedly at the movies one night – with yet another woman he had broken up with – that he had nothing left to teach me. There was great freedom in that realization.

I worked with my Guides to end our teaching soul mate relationship that night during meditation. It was easy to make the change as it no longer served me.

I was thrilled I was finally healing by leaps and bounds, allowing me to once again clearly hear my intuition, my Guides and even the voice of God at times.

As Gwen, I would finally understand the deep symbolism of the red roses William gave Ann – the floriography, or meaning of flowers based on their color.

***

Floriography originated in Persia at a time when women were purposefully kept illiterate, as knowledge is power.

Red roses universally represent love and passion to most people. They were not an appropriate gift for a 17th century married Sea Captain to give to a teenaged girl half his age.

Those roses were a manipulative gift filled with false promise, whether William was aware of it or not.

***

Lance gave me red roses again in 2011. Several years later I understood why that simple gift of no-occasion roses so moved me. He was honoring not only my name, but another of our shared past lives.

We had known each other at the Egyptian Temple of Isis at Philae 2,000 years earlier. My name was Mary, and I was again in my late teens like at Plimoth.

Red roses are Mary Magdalen's energy signature. It took my breath away when I finally connected the puzzle pieces Spirit had patiently been feeding me over time.

I tried to block the possibility of a past life as Mary Magdalen for about a year when it first began presenting, but the memories and experiences continued.

That life initially felt too large and important to believe, particularly after being shown the possibility of other Biblical, historical and famous past lives.

I tried to deny my own inner knowing and deepest truth. That led to increasing health and emotional issues which is a sign of not being on our life path.

I didn't feel worthy of a life with Yeshua ben Joseph (Jesus), just like Lance struggled to accept the possibility he may have been William Shakespeare.

I didn't have enough self-acceptance – my life lesson to master. I feared ridicule and that my ego was out-of-balance, but the evidence kept building.

Multiple healers and psychic friends gently verified my past life as Mary Magdalen without my even asking the question! They offered help and support without my ever mentioning I felt I might have been Magdalen.

Spirit was working overtime to get me the verification and the healing I so desperately needed.

I was deeply concerned with this past life possibility because of how Mary Magdalen has been vilified by so many, including being unfairly branded as a prostitute rather than as the 13th Apostle, and because of the strong martyrdom and victim energy I sensed.

***

The fear of that past life became close to paralyzing. This can occur when we try to deny strong past life energy that is consciously presenting to be released.

I had frozen hips and major mobility issues for several years. It was difficult to walk more than a few steps without severe pain. I had severe stigmata in both hands, wrists and feet and endured multiple wrist and foot surgeries.

I was petrified to have to experience the crucifixion again as I was quickly learning how incredibly powerful my abilities are to vision past life memories.

I didn't feel I had the courage as I could only see the pain of that life, not the privilege, the happiness, and the great love that were also an integral part of the timeline many consider the greatest mystery on Earth.

***

I told Lance regretfully several times I must lack courage.

He shook his head firmly one night and replied, 'You don't lack courage. You've proven yourself again and again. What you lack is trust. What are you going to do about your lack of trust in yourself and perhaps in God or a Higher Power is more the pivotal question.'

His clarity in helping frame that crucial question helped me free myself over the next few years. I moved into not only my life purpose work, but into my larger soul mission across all space and time, and eventually into my legacy work to bring in additional Light for mankind.

I knew we had chosen to incarnate into the Yeshua ben Joseph timeline to bring Light to the planet at an exceptionally dark time when many were enslaved.

Arguably we are back at that same critical juncture in the twenty-first century. There are now more people enslaved or sex-trafficked than in the history of mankind.

***

But how could I trust in the Divine if I had been Mary Magdalen and possibly experienced the crucifixion first-hand?

And what had been my relationship with Yeshua ben Joseph (later called Jesus), if we even had a relationship?

I worked hard to shove the lid back on Pandora's Box – which of course is impossible – or at least to somehow slow down or contain the energy until I had the right energetic healer to help me.

I wouldn't begin to understand the answers to these pivotal questions until the summer of 2014 when I would have two more Quantum Healing Hypnotherapy sessions.

During these lengthy comprehensive sessions Ascended Masters Yeshua ben Joseph and his wife Ascended Master Mary Magdalen came through for me in the most marvelous way possible.

Those two sessions form the basis of 'The Flow III: Mary Magdalen Remembers' which will come later in this trilogy.

Chapter 8

I return now to my life as Anna Warren at the New Colony. My life without one charlatan William Pierce!

I agreed to be courted by a new arrival from the Lyon in 1632. John Totman was ten years older than me and earnestly seeking a wife. I turned that good man down as gently as possible after a lovely carriage ride together.

I knew he wasn't the right man for me from his energy and our single kiss as we rode past the cornfields. Fortunately, I was able to choose my husband that lifetime, which has not always been the case.

My spurned suitor settled in what would become Roxbury, north of Plimoth Plantation. Roxbury later became the south side of Boston.

I don't know what happened to John after he left for Boston, other than a rumor he had not married, which was unusual in our day.

***

I learned in 2013 I made a soul contract with John Totman's soul after we met at the Colony in the 1600s.

The contract we made at Home was for 'a long-term marriage that we will both grow from, and to have beautiful children together.'

We fulfilled our contract for marriage beginning in 1989. This allowed my ghost from my life at Plimoth Plantation to present for help getting to the Light.

I know this all sounds so fantastical. Mark Twain said, 'Truth is stranger than fiction, because fiction is required to stick to possibilities whereas truth is not.'

I feel so much lighter and well-balanced now that I've assembled all these puzzle pieces. It's taken me almost thirty years to do so as it was a complex mystery spanning hundreds of years and multiple lifetimes.

My husband Jake and I were together for almost twenty years. We are blessed with two kind, intelligent, hard-working, lovely daughters, fulfilling our contract for 'a long-term marriage with beautiful children.'

***

I met Lance – formerly William Pierce - in 2010. We began our contract for me to spiritually awaken via his recommending Dr. Michael Newton's 'Journey of Souls.'

I knew immediately it was vital I have both a Past-Life Regression and a Life-Between-Lives four-hour hypnotherapy. Lance recommended the perfect Newton-trained therapist and drove me to and from both sessions in 2011 and 2012. They changed my life!

In 2013, I fully integrated Ann with my Future Self Gwendolyn. Gwen began raising her vibration to 5D and higher, including aligning with her Higher Self, as well as into her I AM presence, also called the Christ Consciousness.

She began training to help others heal and release pain and other energy that no longer serves them, and to manage their own energy and spiritual awakening. The path requires tremendous growth and at times sacrifice but is also incredibly magical and rewarding. With great gifts comes great responsibility.

***

We return once again to the seventeenth century. I'm delighted to report I finally found romantic love as Ann Warren, my fondest wish for that lifetime!

Thomas Little arrived at Plimoth on a supply ship in 1632. I had been at Plimoth for almost a decade.

Thomas was three years older than me. He was a barrister from Devon County, England and would become the Colony's first attorney.

Thomas built a small home for himself immediately upon arrival. This was unusual for a single man, but he would need quiet, private space to serve as the settlement's first barrister.

We married in 1633 after first becoming great friends and then enjoying a suitable courtship. We had a great deal in common. My family accepted Thomas readily, which was a tremendous blessing for me.

I am so fortunate I deeply loved and was loved by my husband that lifetime. What can be more important than mutual respect, trust and love in your closest personal relationships?

***

Thomas sold his dwelling house to Richard Higgins for twenty-one bushels of corn when we married. This allowed us to build a larger home closer to my family and to the trading post.

We married at the Plantation meetinghouse fort on April 19th, 1633 after several months of planning. Our marriage was celebrated by the entire Colony.

I still remember our wedding feast of pasty venison, my favorite type of deer delicacy, along with roasted venison, Thomas' favorite. We also had tiny early grapes, carefully gathered diverse prize plums and nuts as well as fresh-baked breads. And our omnipresent maize, prepared many ways.

We built a much larger daub and wattle wooden home with room for Thomas to work from home. We prayed for a large family to bless our union over time.

***

Robert Bartlett married my beloved eldest sister Mary in 1630. He was twenty-six years of age and Mary aged twenty-one when they married after having met as teenagers.

On May 28th, 1635, Thomas gifted some of his land to Robert to help Mary and Robert establish their own household.

I recognized Robert in the future at our shared workplace when I was Gwen. His name was very similar to when we were at Plimoth, but more importantly, I recognized his energy. It was a lovely feeling to find someone with whom you've had positive lifetimes.

Robert had emigrated aboard the Anne of London with my sisters, Elizabeth and me in 1623. Mary and Robert had eight children over time and both lived a long, full life.

My sister Mary and my brother-in-law's bodies were interred at Burial Hill in Plymouth, now called White Horse Cemetery.

Gwen visited White Horse Cemetery in July of 2014 and left red roses by the Bartlett marker. The large cemetery has numerous Bartlett family stones.

My next younger sister Sarah married John Cooke in 1634 and had five children.

My next-to-youngest sister Elizabeth married Richard Church in 1635 and had a large brood of eleven children. My nephew Benjamin Church would later become infamous during King Philip's War.

I so loved being an aunt, as well as a mother! Our baby sister Abigail who had been so seasick during our long passage to the Colony married Anthony Snow in 1639. Abigail and Anthony had six children.

My younger brother Nathaniel, born at Plimoth in 1624, married Sarah Walker in 1645 and had an astonishing twelve children. He died young in 1667.

Our youngest brother Joseph was born in 1626 in Plimoth, and married Priscilla Faunce in 1653. They had six children.

Clearly, we Warrens had a remarkably large family within a short generation or two.

The Richard and Elizabeth Warren line became the most prolific of the Plimoth Plantation families. We have an estimated 20,000 descendants.

***

1633 was memorable not only for Thomas and my wedding, but for an outbreak of disease that killed many Native people and about twenty Colonists. The population of the Colony was approximately four hundred at the time, a decade after my arrival.

We had expanded beyond the town of Plimoth by 1633 – including across the Bay to Mattakesett, which became Duxbury. Some men were granted land at Conahasset, known as Green's Harbor, and later Marshfield.

As our population grew, another trading house was built on the Connecticut River at Matianuck, which later became Windsor, Connecticut.

Our early expansions were peaceful. But in later years the increased contact between the Native Wampanoag and the English Colonists led to friction, ultimately resulting in King Philip's War of 1675 to 1676.

Plimoth lost all four of our trading houses in the years 1634 to 1636 as we were becoming a backwater due to our shallow harbor, especially in comparison to Boston. Other settlements were becoming much larger.

Duxburrow became Duxbury and incorporated in 1637. In 1636 Connecticutis was settled by Colonists from Massachusetts Bay.

As our English population increased, we Colonists pushed out in every direction, as far as to what would become Cape Cod. We established additional towns which filled in the map right back to where we had originally landed in 1620 on the tip of the Cape at Provincetown.

We outbred the Natives, as well as had more people arriving by ships in greater numbers than the Natives could increase their population.

**

In 1636 to 1638, war with the Pequots and the English occurred in Connecticut. Hundreds of Natives died.

Plimoth Plantation was not directly involved, but the war set the increasingly tense tone for future English and Native relations.

Taunton became recognized in the Plimoth Court records in 1636 to 1637. Ten men from Saugus, a small town to our north, received permission to settle in Plimoth County and chose the future Sandwich on Cape Cod.

In 1638, Yarmouth is mentioned for the first time and in 1638 to 1639, Barnstable. This brought increased contact and eventually bloody conflict with the Natives in 1675 to 1676.

The Great Migration of the early-to-mid 1600s brought over 7000 families from England to the New World. There were over 250 voyages in total.

Captain William Pierce became known as 'The Ferryman of the North.' He was the most traveled Sea Captain of our time.

Lance remains an avid world traveler today and is employed in the transportation industry, so is always on the move.

**

Now that I have provided the larger historical backdrop to our time, I return to the narration of my life with my husband. I was twenty-two when we married in 1633 and Thomas aged twenty-five.

During our long and rewarding marriage of more than three decades, Thomas and I were blessed with nine children! I cannot fully express what great joy our large family brought to our hearts.

Our seven oldest offspring were born in Plimoth and our two youngest in what is now Marshfield. Town lines often change as the years roll by.

Thomas and I welcomed our first child when I was twenty-three years of age, and had our last when I was forty-five. The timing with Plimoth losing our trading post was perfect as I quickly became too busy with my growing family to easily work there as I had for so many years.

Our oldest daughter sadly pre-deceased me by fifteen years. Two more of our children died during King Philip's War.

So many died then, both we English, including Captain Michael Pierce, William's youngest brother, but even more of the Indians.

What happened to that wonderful, proud honorable race in just fifty short years from the Colonial settling of America was devastating. The Wampanoag had been on that land for as long as twelve thousand years.

Twelve thousand years! A long and proud history was essentially wiped away in five decades.

***

I return to my tale of Thomas and my children. A year after our marriage, our first child was born in 1634. We named her Abigail, like my baby sister.

Abigail is from the Old Testament and means 'My Father is Joy.' Abigail married Josiah Keen in 1656 at twenty-two, the same age as when I married Thomas. They graced us with two grandchildren. Sadly, their oldest daughter died young, as was too common an occurrence in our day.

Abigail, our beloved eldest daughter died in her twenties in 1660, but she gave birth first to a second child in 1655. Abigail and Josiah named their son Josiah Keen, Junior.

Josiah later married Hannah Dingley as his second wife. They had seven children. Thomas and I considered them our grandchildren. Every life was precious, and we had an immensely strong sense of family and community.

Our second daughter Ruth was born in 1636. Ruth is a Biblical name from the Hebrew meaning 'Friend or Companion.' Ruth did not marry. She died on February 19th, 1676 during King Philip's War.

It bears repeating an estimated 600 Colonists died out of a total of 3,500 during Philip's war, and a devastating 3,000 of the 3,400 Natives, with the remainder sold into slavery.

That still brings tears to my eyes today and I feel some shame.

Our third daughter Hannah was born in 1638. The Aramaic meaning for Hannah is 'Grace.' Hannah married Stephen Tilden on January 25th, 1661 in the lovely waterfront town of Scituate.

Aramaic was the language spoken during the time of Christ. I wonder if I had some memory I used to speak Aramaic two thousand years earlier during Yeshua ben Joseph's lifetime?

Hannah and Stephen had twelve children of their own, impressive progeny even by Warren-Little standards. Both lived a good long life.

On March 12th, 1638 William Taylor transferred his indenture from Mr. John Atwood to Thomas. We needed help to grow more food for our burgeoning family.

Our fourth daughter Patience was born in 1640. Some thought we named her for the Latin 'to suffer,' but I prefer the Old French meaning 'to endure.' Patience married Joseph Jones on November 11th, 1657, farther north in Weymouth. They had another large family of ten children and settled later in Hingham.

They named their oldest child Sarah. I was pleased to have a Sarah granddaughter. Both Patience and Joseph lived a good long life, like Hannah and Stephen.

I have named my daughters Sarah in several of my lives, including my youngest Sar'h-Tamar when I was Mary Magdalen, and again during the American Civil War when I was Dolly Sumner Lunt Burge. I was fortunate to meet her again this lifetime – I feel the same soul was my daughter Sarah twice.

***

Immigration slowed in 1640 and abruptly ended our lucrative cattle trade to the Massachusetts Bay Colonists. Large-scale migration to New England ended in the years 1640 to 1660 due to Puritan success in the English Civil War.

Many New Englanders, including our Plimoth Colony Governor Edward Winslow, returned to England.

Seconk was first mentioned in Court records in 1642, and in 1645 it became Rehoboth. Seconk would later become a flashpoint during King Philip's War.

Mercy was born in 1644, our fifth and final daughter. Mercy means 'giving thanks or forgiveness.' We lost two pregnancies between Patience and Mercy, hence her name.

Mercy married John Sawyer in November of 1666 in Marshfield. She was another twenty-two-year-old bride in our family. Mercy and John had seven children, and then sadly we lost our precious daughter to childbirth fever.

After Mercy passed on, John remarried Rebecca Barker Snow. They had ten more children.

We again considered that next large brood our grandchildren, and you begin to have an idea of how immense our family was becoming in two short generations. We no longer needed Mayflower ships to build the population at the rate we reproduced.

The Richard and Elizabeth Warren family descendants now number about 20,000, as stated earlier. Some names you will recognize include Civil War general and President Ulysses Grant, President Franklin Delano Roosevelt, Alan Shepherd, Jr. – the first American in space and one of the first to walk on the moon – and actor Richard Gere.

***

Thomas and I began to have sons after I gave birth to five daughters. This was like my birth family – five sisters and later two younger brothers.

Isaac was born in 1646. His name means 'laughter' from the Book of Genesis. He married Bethia Thomas in 1674, and they had twelve children. Isaac died in Marshfield in 1699, and Bethia two decades later in Pembroke in 1718.

I attended their funerals as a ghost. I was still Earth-bound energy after dropping my body in 1676. Once you return Home to heal, you may visit Earth as a Spirit.

I read Isaac and Bethia's headstones. I read so many headstones of my family during the previous three hundred years. I so wish they would standardize the information engraved on them!

I strongly prefer the ones with full detail – middle names, full dates of birth and death. Even someone with 'The Memory' like me cannot remember all this wonderful family history easily.

I had to look some of these dates up, as guided by Spirit, to complete this narrative as accurately as possible.

We welcomed our second son – our seventh child – with as much joy as we welcomed our first baby. We named him Ephraim. He was born on May 17th, 1650, when I was becoming an older mother at age thirty-nine.

Ephraim means 'fruitful.' He married Mary Sturtevant on November 22nd, 1672, and they had nine children. Isaac died on November 24th, 1717 in Scituate. Mary died earlier that year on February 10th, 1717, also in Scituate.

Our son Thomas Junior was born in 1654. Thomas is Aramaic for 'twin.' He did not marry. He died in Pawtucket, Rhode Island, on March 26th, 1676, during King Philip's War.

Our youngest child was a son born in 1656. We named our ninth child Samuel from the Hebrew. It means 'he who listens to God,' which I thought was fitting. Samuel married Sarah Gray on May 18th, 1682 in Marshfield. Another Sarah, like my sister and granddaughter.

Samuel and Sarah had four children. I was present for their wedding and each child's birth. I can only hope they felt my loving presence as I had dropped my body in 1676.

Samuel died in Bristol, Rhode Island on January 16th, 1707. Sarah died on February 14th, St. Valentine's Day, in 1736. She also died in Bristol almost three decades later.

I was forty-five when Samuel was born, and Thomas forty-eight. No more children came to Thomas and me after Samuel as I was no longer of child-bearing age.

We had nine children, fifty-six grandchildren and seventeen honorary grandchildren from when two of our sons-in-law remarried. We also had forty-eight nieces and nephews from my side of the family alone.

***

My story as Ann Warren Little – my experiences, my life at Plimoth and elsewhere – may not always match the historical narrative. There are also discrepancies in recorded history.

For example, Gwen was unable to find any record of Plimoth Plantation homes with back bedrooms – all appeared to be single room cottages. But she clearly saw two tiny bedrooms that she and her four sisters shared during her past-life regression, so that is what we wrote.

'To thine own self be true.' (William Shakespeare)

I purposefully do not research or read about a potential past life until my own memories are solid and in writing as I don't want to be influenced by outside sources.

I believe historical discrepancies occur in part because other souls have chosen to experience a life as Ann Warren Little at Plimoth, as well as Mary Magdalen, and some may be doing so NOW, given that time is continuous vs. linear.

Time is better described as a loop than a line. It's a complex reality we simplify as 'past-present-future' to more easily understand it with our limited human brains.

Hence the written records have discrepancies, but portions may be accurate for each of the different Ann Warren Littles born in England who then emigrated to the New World in the 1620s.

***

Thomas became the Marshfield Constable on June 3rd, 1662. We sold our property in South Plymouth. We moved to the former farm of Major William Holmes, who had passed on, and made many improvements to that property.

Thomas became known as 'Thomas Little of the Yele (or Eel) River' when he attended town meetings. The Eel River was near Indian Brook. The word 'El' also refers to God, our Divine Father.

Thomas served on the Plimoth Grand Jury in June of 1664. He was on the Plimoth Colony list of men able – required, more accurately – to bear arms.

We had our large family and many good friends and congenial neighbors as we were still a small Colony.

Unfortunately, we had bad blood with a few individuals, typically due to the nature of Thomas' work as a barrister, but most notably with Captain Myles Standish.

I need to own my part here, as Captain Shrimp and I did not get along. It is amazing how energy can still need to be released so many lifetimes later.

Captain Myles Standish died peacefully at home on his Duxbury farm in 1656. He was in his early seventies and had spent the last twenty years of his life more as an advisor to the Colony than as a soldier.

Myles Standish is considered a brave hero by many. Yet I was not the only moderate at Plimoth who found him incredibly arrogant in many of his actions and barbaric toward the Indians.

***

I greatly disliked his chauvinistic attitude toward women. Standish made clear his opinion regarding Abby and me running the trading post. He belittled our ability to do so competently, as well as the trading post's contribution to the Colony's economy.

I'll let the facts speak for themselves. By 1627, four years after my arrival and seven years after the original Mayflower ship in 1620, we had made enough trades of corn for beaver skins to pay off the Adventurers, our London-based financiers who funded the Colony.

This was no small accomplishment. I was sixteen years of age in 1627, and Abby was fourteen or fifteen. We ran the trading post essentially on our own. Our commerce made an important contribution to paying off the entire Plantation's debt.

Personally, I would have been delighted to trade Standish for a single skimpy – make that shrimpy – beaver skin, or half-filled, wormy bushel of corn!

All trades considered. He truly was an arsworm. I trust you'll be able to translate that pejorative to its modern-day equivalent.

I find it intriguing Abby and I re-met this lifetime at work in 1998 when I was working in sales, and she was later employed in sales, too. We were once again co-workers engaged in commerce. She also had the same last name she did at the New Colony, which helped me recognize her from that life.

***

I return to my favorite topic, our children. Thomas and my children had grown into such marvelous adults – they made my heart sing! All but two married as mentioned earlier and had large families of their own.

Thomas and I remained so happy together as man and wife and were as thrilled with our grandchildren as we were with our children and their spouses.

The years sped by. I was joyous with my lot in life.

But then Thomas passed on quite suddenly at age sixty-four. I wasn't prepared for my husband to go Home so abruptly. I didn't handle his passing well.

We buried Thomas with great sadness at the Winslow Cemetery on March 12th, 1672. That cemetery is now known as the Old Winslow Burying Ground in Marshfield as Governor Edward Winslow is buried there, too.

The administration of Thomas' estate passed to me on August 14th, 1672. I was named in Thomas' will, as were our children, our grandson John Jones, and Thomas' servant Sarah Bonney.

I lived alone as a widow in my early sixties for a few years after Thomas' death. I had no interest in remarrying, which was unusual in our day.

I acquired a spunky black tomcat for company. That same soul has reincarnated with me many times as my energetic protector and companion. He's now Gwen's cat Midnight.

***

Midnight and I found each other again in the early 2000s. He was adopted from a local cat shelter when he positively launched himself into a surprised Gwen's arms. He raced in from a back room, jumped up onto an empty wheeled chair at the front desk, setting it spinning, and then up onto the counter. The tiny kitten launched himself at Gwen's chest so quickly his family didn't see him coming! Fortunately, Gwen caught him gently with both hands when he landed on her.

The kitten's soul recognized Gwen's energy, though he was only six weeks old and was neutered that morning. It was clear he had chosen his family.

Gwen's six and eight-year-old daughters renamed the tiny black and white kitten Midnight. He was so small Jake was able to hold him fully spread out in one hand.

In addition to our shared life at Plimoth, I believe Midnight was a temple cat at the Egyptian Temple of Isis, and a magical deer on Gwen's current property when she lived on it previously as a Native and is most often a large guard dog or a black panther including having possibly been a panther in the Garden of Eden.

***

Gwen received closure for Thomas' death more than three hundred years later. She had an amazing surprise discovery at the Old Winslow Burying Grounds during her July 2014 trip to Boston.

Gwen found her name 'Ann' below the inscription 'Thomas Little' on a large monument commemorating the Town of Marshfield founders.

She unexpectedly burst into tears and left the bouquet of red roses she was carrying at the base of that monument, not having known why her Guides asked her to bring flowers.

Gwen had not known why she was to go to Marshfield. My Future Self finally realized she was to find the cemetery to pay her respects to her own past life and to her husband's.

This was powerful energetic closure for a woman who had been a ghost for hundreds of years. She finally felt heard, as well as recognized, as Ann Warren Little.

Gwen understood me well in my Ann Warren Little because Gwen is a fellow romantic, as is Lance. This is the reason Lance and Gwen were able to help me get Home in 2013 whereas they were not successful in other lives together in the interim. I'm grateful to them both!

***

I wish to pay special tribute to my stepmother Elizabeth Walker Warren. She lived from 1583 to 1673 and is now Gwen's mother as I have stated earlier in my memoir.

Due to her remarkably long life of ninety years, Elizabeth Warren died in Plimoth just a year before my husband Thomas and only a few years before my own death. I'm glad Elizabeth didn't live to see King Philip's War.

She was an incredible mother, friend, protector, and staunch supporter to my sisters and me in every way possible, as well as to our younger brothers Nathaniel and Joseph.

Elizabeth equally embraced our husbands, wives and children – her grandchildren – and then her great-grandchildren. My stepmother lived to see at least seventy-five of her great-grandchildren.

She had a tremendous sense of family both at the New Colony and again today.

For five twice-orphaned girls, Elizabeth was the bedrock of our world. She was the best of the Plimoth Plantation energy. We are deeply grateful to her then and now.

Elizabeth stood out as a strong individual, rare in a time when women were more often simply a reflection of their husbands and children.

***

The Plymouth County Records paid her the following tribute:

'Mistris Elizabeth Warren, an aged widow, aged above 90 yeares, deceased on the second of October, 1673, who having lived a godly life, came to her grave as a shocke of corn, fully ripe.'

Our stepmother was a remarkable woman for her times, including being prosperous in managing her lands. Unlike most Plimoth widows, she was not obliged to remarry, which was unusual as she was only in her forties when Father died.

Elizabeth was customarily given the title of 'Mrs.,' when most women were simply called 'Goodwife.' Can you feel the energy and status difference?

She was also honored by being allowed to succeed to her husband's rights as 'Purchaser.' Her name appears frequently in the Colonial records for she had the rare distinction of remaining a widow for over four decades.

Her will is recorded in Suffolk County Probate Records V.:11. Her estate was 365 pounds, 14 shillings.

This equates to $480 US dollars as of September 2018. My sense is that may be a significant estate for the time as more than thirty years have passed.

Chapter 9

Friction increased between we Colonists and the Natives during the 1650s and 1660s, and certainly after Thomas and Elizabeth's deaths. War doesn't typically break out overnight.

English expansion into Native territory, though done by purchase, brought our livestock into proximity with Native fields. Incidents of livestock trespass and damage became common.

Resentments arose from the next generation of Natives regarding the low prices we were paying for land. The younger Indians saw the writing on the wall they weren't going to be able to sustain themselves as they had for thousands of years.

On May 9th, 1657, Governor William Bradford died. He had been our governor for approximately three decades. Thomas Prence was elected governor at the June Court.

By June 1660, the great Sachem Native leader Massasoit had also dropped his body. Upon the death of his father Massasoit, Wamsutta asked to change his name according to the custom of the Natives.

Wamsutta requested and received English names for himself and his younger brother Metacomet from the Plimoth Court. The brothers became known as Alexander and Phillip.

Am I the only one who finds it demeaning a Native man had to petition the English Colonial Court to follow his own people's custom?

***

Alexander died under suspicious circumstances in the summer of 1662. Poison was suspected, but if that were true, poison from whom, and for what purpose?

Philip succeeded his older brother as Sachem.

Controversy developed between Philip and the Plimoth government in August to September of 1671 when the English government attempted to confiscate the weapons of the Pokanoket, Philip's people.

On September 29th, 1671, Philip signed a new treaty, promising obedience to the Plimoth government. Take a moment to fully consider what that must have felt like.

What were Philip's motives? What about his hopes, his dreams for himself, his family and his people?

Over time, the Natives were unable to live by our heavy-handed English Colonist rules. We eradicated first their culture, and eventually them as a people, in fifty short years of Colonial history.

We obliterated a twelve-thousand-year-old people, in a mere five decades...

I find that horrifying, particularly as I remember numerous Native lives of my own, including having been Wampanoag in what is now the state of Massachusetts.

***

On March 29th, 1673, Governor Thomas Prence passed on. Josiah Winslow succeeded him as Governor.

On June 20th, 1675, 'The Great Indian War,' which later became known as 'King Philip's War,' began with an attack by some Wampanoag on Swansea.

In July of 1675, war spread quickly with attacks on Colonials in Taunton, Middleboro, and Dartmouth.

The Natives guerilla warfare style was initially highly successful as it would be again centuries later in Vietnam.

Guerilla warfare confounded we English. We had the wrong equipment, training, and mindset for a man-to-man ground fight. We only knew how to march across open fields in straight, steady lines, as was the infantry of our time in Europe.

My perception is the wise old Native men desired peace. But Philip and the other young leaders and warriors would not hear of it. They had experienced enough of the severity of the white Colonists, numerous executions, and already the selling of their captured loved ones.

Peace in the form of arguably unjust punishments, slavery, and humiliating submission to the English was too high a price to pay.

I don't know which Native man said, 'Let us live as long as we can, and die like men, and not live to be enslaved,' but it reflected the resolve of many of their younger Sachem.

***

Unfortunately, I wouldn't live long enough to raise my etheric sword of peace to help build and sustain the Heaven on Earth energy for mankind. But my soul would learn and remember and would seek to build the energies of love and of peace again in a future Golden Age.

I would do so as Gwen three hundred years later. She would be handed an etheric sword in 2017 as one of the last steps to become a Certified Spiritual Teacher.

Gwen asked her Guides carefully if she was to accept the sword as she had been told to 'lay down her sword' from her many warrior and ruler type lives. She had finally learned just because someone offers you something does not mean you should accept it until you are clear it's for your highest and holiest.

Her Guides told her to put on her best dress. She immediately saw herself in a gorgeous low-cut, long green silk dress. The dress became part of Mother Earth.

She raised the sword high above her head as a Sword of Peace. The Light from it glinted first around the Earth, and then into the galaxy. It was the only sword she would ever touch again. It was the only way she would use a sword as she incarnated to help restore peace through the galaxies.

***

King Philip sold off a great deal of land to purchase English weapons. His planned strategy was to take back his people's lands by force.

Wars will continue to erupt until we master the lesson that we truly are ONE race – the human race. We need to move from the scarcity mindset to one of abundance.

Attacks on Lancaster and Concord were only the beginning. Deadly fighting spread amazingly quickly to so many locations. It was a terrifying time as towns and solitary farms alike were suddenly attacked by fearsome Native warriors.

At the Rowlandson Garrison, fifty or so men and women were awakened one morning by two uniquely terrifying sounds – the loud, whooping Indian war cry, which is both bone-chilling and unforgettable, and the firing of guns.

Terrified English settlers looked out from the Rowlandson Garrison to discover their homes in flames. They could see and hear Indians in the first dim light of dawn massacring their families, friends and neighbors with both tomahawks and rifles.

Mrs. Rowlandson and her son and daughter were captured during the melee with the hope of ransoming them. We later learned from Mrs. Rowlandson's diary that she and her children were generally treated with kindness.

She described her Native captors as being 'many hundred, old and young, some sick, and some lame. Many had papooses on their backs.'

Imagine the horror of an entire people having to constantly move around in unsafe conditions, increasingly hungry, with the most defenseless of your loved ones with you? It still brings me to tears, hundreds of years later.

The torture of Englishmen by the Indians was the exception rather than the rule. Our women and children especially were spared, whereas we settlers slew without regard to age or gender and were bloody self-righteous in our torturing.

We were following the European soldiery of our time – spare no enemy, though I am unclear how an unarmed man, woman or child is an enemy.

Where was our humanity? Did we not truly believe in 'Love Thy Neighbor' when sorely tested?

We would not have survived at the New Colony without the Indians many kindnesses in teaching us how to farm that rocky land and how to survive in an area that could be inhospitable.

***

Gwen still experiences chills over three hundred years later simply writing about the whooping Indian war cry. Writing is therapeutic for her, as it is for many, regardless if it is publicly shared.

Writing is an excellent tool to heal and release old energy that no longer serves you. You may choose to gently tear up or burn the pages to complete the process if you are not guided to file them away or to share them publicly.

Gwen had PTSD (Post-Traumatic Stress Disorder) in her central nervous system not only from Plimoth, but from many lives as a Warrior and a Ruler. Many people do, as it can be from any lifetime or be cumulative across many incarnations.

Past-Life Regression can be therapeutic for healing chronic physical or emotional pain, anxiety and panic attacks, depression, PTSD, disorders, disease, and to unblock creativity and self-limiting beliefs.

***

I return now to the winter of 1675 to 1676. We had done a fine job of supplying the Natives with guns with which to attack us.

What were we thinking? Why do we still follow this practice throughout the world today? The issue is more complex than war being a highly profitable business.'

The United States spent an estimated fifty-four percent of its discretionary spending on military expenditures in 2015, according to NationalPriorities.org. Discretionary spending is about one-third of the nation's total budget. If you look at the US military spending as part of the GDP (Gross Domestic Product), we spend several orders of magnitude more on defense than the second highest spender. How do we change this current reality?

The film 'Captain Phillips' (starring Tom Hanks) has similar energy to King Philip's War. Four desperately poor teenaged Somali pirates hijack the Alabama – an unarmed American supply ship – with illegal arms purchased from a foreign government.

Abduwali Muse continues to serve a thirty-three-year sentence in an American federal prison since his 2011 conviction for the 2009 act of piracy and attempted ransoming of Captain Phillips. Muse was the first person charged with piracy in an American court in over one hundred years.

***

I died as Ann Warren Little on my home's tiny front stoop on February 19th, 1676 during King Philip's War.

My death on my own threshold was typical for that terrifying time. The Indians would silently enter a town during the dark of night. They were soundless, expert hunters and completely one with the terrain.

The Natives would hide in the brush, behind our orchard walls, barns and outhouses. Suddenly, from all sides would come the hair-raising war cries from attacking Indians!

We Planters would sometimes hear the petrified cries and moans of our neighbors, friends and family. We were completely surprised and utterly horrified by the attacks as the war continued to spread shockingly quickly.

By the time you heard the chilling war whoops, it was much too late to say goodbye or make your peace with God.

The silence was deafening after all had been slain, left for dead, or a select few carried off for ransom.

The silver cord severed when my physical body was no longer viable. My soul then left the body.

After my soul floated up above my broken body, one of my first thoughts was what happened to my many loved ones? I had so many beloved children, sons-in-law, daughters-in-law and grandchildren living at Plimoth. Lifetime friends and neighbors, too.

The carnage was so fast-moving and chaotic I couldn't easily understand what happened to whom – who lived and who died that day, both settlers and Natives?

I didn't understand I'd be able to easily learn that at Home at the right time. I so needed to go Home to regain the higher soul-level perspective.

Instead, I waited for William Pierce.

It can be difficult to grasp that we only bring a portion of our energy with us to any incarnation. This is true for all souls, but my choice to remain behind as a ghost – as Earth-bound energy – after my death was more unusual.

Normally the portion of energy that has just left the body returns to Source and reunites with the full soul essence.

I trust I learned and grew from my long tenure as a ghost. I have no intent to glamorize or recommend a choice born in fear and confusion and then continued for hundreds of years due to incredible stubbornness and heartbreak, combined with an inability to forgive.

***

My impression is the few settlers who made it to the garrison house determined who lived and who died during the brutal attack of February 19th, 1676.

I asked many Native ghosts and spirits after my death as to the fate of my large family and closest friends. I asked about them by name. But the Indians were unable to sort out who was who, as they didn't know most of our names.

I was more recognizable to the Indians than most Englishwomen because of my years in the trading post. Many of them knew my name was Ann Little and that I came from the Warren family whose cottage was closest to the harbor.

Again, the answer to any question in the Universe was readily available at Home as was profound healing. But I couldn't seem to remember these critical facts.

I also was too stubborn to go, as I insisted on waiting for William when Guides and Angels came to help me find my way Home. He said he would return for me, and I believed him.

Fixating too much energy on events of the past rather than looking forward and up to the Light may lead to becoming Earth-bound. Lower vibration emotions including anger, regret or shame or an unhealthy fixation on unfinished business are major causes of a soul becoming stuck as a ghost.

*I highly recommend Donya Wicken's **TheZenofBen.com** It's a wonderful resource to help stuck souls – disincarnated energy, or ghosts – cross over to the Light.*

***

I learned what happened to my son Thomas Little and to William's brother Michael Pierce because those two deaths became well-known, as did my nephew Benjamin Church's wartime actions.

I'll begin with Benjamin. My nephew became famous as an advisor to Governor Josiah Winslow during the war.

I'll be blunt. I love Benjamin at the soul level but was sickened by his actions helping set fire to the largest Wampanoag fort. It was known to be filled with many Native women, children, injured and elderly.

It was morally wrong on every level. But it was a time of war. Bedrock values change quickly.

Settlers and soldiers alike were shot down on our thresholds by arrow or rifle, and our homes were set ablaze.

In Dedham, Massachusetts – where my Future Self Gwendolyn would have the good fortune to marry Jake at the lovely Endicott Estate, a National Historic Registry site – most of the settlers and troops reached the garrison house. We English began firing the cannon to signal the attack.

I heard after my death that the Indians drew back across the river for safety after the initial onslaught and burned the bridge behind them. The Natives posted a note on what was now the settler's side.

They promised to war for twenty-one years if they were provoked further. The Indians stated they had nothing to lose but their lives, whereas we settlers would lose our homes and cattle, too.

The Natives gambled that would make us back down as we had more to lose. Yet those who have the most to lose can instead determine who will fight and with how much vehemence.

***

Weymouth was attacked on February 25th, 1676. On March 12th, 1676, William Clark's garrison house in Plimoth was attacked when the men marched in line to church – Captain Standish style – that Sunday morning. Eleven were massacred, Bibles and rifles in hand.

By March 14th, 1676, a large force of the Valley Indians attacked North Hampton. That spring was filled with a palpable sense of fear.

We could not work our fields without being guarded by our neighbors and soldiers. We had to tend our stock one-handed, arms in hand, like we worshipped for my lifetime at the New Colony.

Food became scarce for we Planters. It was in desperate short supply for the Indians as they were waging a moving war.

The steep price of that strategy was they were not staying anywhere long enough to grow food and were unable to hunt, fish, forage or steal enough food to feed over three thousand mouths.

Families who lived on the outskirts of town were too frightened to occupy their homes. Even in the villages, many were now sleeping in the garrisons every night. Two or more guards were placed in the stockades.

From the Connecticut Valley, east as far as Plimoth and Providence, the war parties from the tribes dispensed death and destruction to we Colonials.

***

Our son Thomas died March 26th, 1676 at Pawtucket, Rhode Island during King Philip's War at Rehoboth.

Thomas was a soldier in Captain Moseley's Company. He was captured and taken to an Indian encampment, later returned, and shortly thereafter killed in battle.

Thomas Junior left a will dated February 19th, 1675. His heirs included his siblings Samuel, Hannah, Patience, Mercy and me – his mother Anna – as he was not married.

Thomas did not know I pre-deceased him a short month earlier. Times were tumultuous during King Philip's War, and communication much more limited than today.

***

Captain Michael Pierce lived in Scituate and was twenty years younger than his brother William. He was dispatched by Captain Amos from Plimoth with fifty soldiers and a group of Indians aligned with the English.

The night before Michael Pierce's death they slept at the Seekonk garrison house. My understanding from the Natives after I dropped my body was Pierce was a bit impetuous. He was lured over the Pawtucket into a position unfavorable for defense.

Captain Pierce realized too late the enemy numbers confronting him and fell back to the river bank. He formed his men into a circle, back-to-back, and fought on in the vain hope that Captain Edmunds, whose assistance he had requested that morning, would come up from Providence as it was only eight miles away.

But it was Sunday, and the messenger chose not to disturb Sunday services. That became a fatal choice for a large company of our men.

Captain Michael Pierce and his men were cut off from all retreat. Pierce's company fell. Almost his entire command was killed or captured.

There is much debate whether nine of the latter were led to a swamp now known as Nine Men's Misery a few miles to the north and whether they were tortured and killed.

125

I simply don't know. I will say that doesn't sound like the many Wampanoag I knew so well as peaceful trading partners and neighbors, but it was a time of war.

Don't forget my nephew Benjamin Church had already set fire to the Wampanoag fort filled with women and children, the elderly and injured, killing hundreds.

My belief is there is much purposeful misinformation and propaganda during wartime. This can be true during times of peace, depending on the government tolerated by the people.

Don Henley of Eagles band fame sings about the government in 'A Month of Sundays,' written in 1984. It's quite pertinent here and worth a listen or read of his lyrics.

Two days after Captain Michael Pierce's company was eliminated, Seekonk was burned by the victorious Natives. Philip's men burned Rehoboth next.

English towns began to refuse to send more troops to fight.

***

I had no way to know this information during my lifetime as Ann Little. But since I stayed so long in the Plimoth Plantation vicinity after my death, I learned and endlessly discussed much history from Colonial America with the Natives for the next three hundred years.

This is one of the reasons I have such detailed first-hand recollections from that life today. I have tried my best to be fair and just in my reporting of events but can only hope to speak my own truth.

***

Remaining 'stuck' in a past life for hundreds of years may be why my Future Self Gwen's Past-Life Regression regarding Plimoth was so detailed, and why so many more memories of that life continued to flood into her conscious mind for years to come.

A typical Past-Life Regression may only need to provide a few snippets of information or images as that's all that's necessary to allow one to heal and release the old emotions to fully embrace their life NOW.

It's all about 'the now' – also known as mindfulness – I believe thought leader Eckhart Tolle has it right.

Beloved spiritual leader Ram Dass hit the nail on the head in 1971 with his seminal text, 'Be Here Now.' It remains a best-selling classic for so many reasons.

We need to trust what we see, hear, feel, smell, taste, touch, or simply know, whether it's during a formal regression or other healing session or in our daily life.

I encourage you to accept these divine insights are for your highest good. If we remember to take a breath of life, learn to balance our egos and put our fears and doubts aside along with self-limiting beliefs, we're much more able to trust, to raise our vibration and enjoy a life of peace, love and joy.

Occasionally an entire book needs to be written to fully heal a past life and to complete a successful soul retrieval back into the proper place in an individual's timeline.

This was my soul's journey with my Colonial American experiences, which also included the Salem Witchcraft Trials.

Another excellent example is 'Lizzy,' written by Laurie Regan. Laurie wrote 'Lizzy' to help people release past life slave energy, especially that of the deep South in the mid-1800s. Look for it on Amazon.

The energy of 'Lizzy' is similar to 'Twelve Years a Slave' and is intense, yet ultimately uplifting.

***

I return to my recounting of King Philip's War. In May of 1676, the remaining houses in Middleboro were torched, more died in Taunton, and parts of Scituate were burned. Communications were severed between Plimoth and Boston.

In July of 1676 one hundred years before our independence from Great Britain, the tide turned.

The Colonists now began to capture or kill the Natives who were desperately short of food from having waged an on-the-move war. The outcome of a war is often determined by the supply chain – in this case, food.

On July 22nd, 1676, the Plimoth Court arranged for many of the Wampanoag children to be placed as servants with Colonial families until they reached the age of twenty-five.

We had officially conquered a proud, honorable people, one who had been both friend and foe. I don't believe this was ever our intent, but we must look truthfully at what occurred, own our part, and do our best to make it right.

It is never too late to honestly attempt to make it right. What should be done about 'Christopher Columbus Day?' Times have changed, and we are wise to change with them, and to work to raise the vibration of that energy.

***

On August 9th, 1676, to my great sadness and shame, Governor Josiah Winslow approved the sale of one hundred Natives as slaves. They were sent to Bermuda.

I don't know which Sea Captain took them. It wasn't William Pierce, though he too, transported slaves as that was somehow acceptable in the 17th century and certainly still happens today.

Eventually thousands of Natives were sold. Reverend John Cotton wrote about the terrifying events of 1676 one year later in March of 1677.

The Reverend wrote, 'Philip's boy now goes to be sold.'

This act of barbarity toward a child and his mother was what the Natives had learned to expect from us. Philip's adored wife and son disappear from the pages of history in 1676 after having survived moving around with him for much of the war.

With them went the lineage of Massasoit. The great Sachem leader had been friends to we English settlers for more than four decades.

***

Gwen noted while writing this book that Lance posted a poignant painting on Facebook regarding the many Irish sold and transported on slave ships.

All of us are working at some level – consciously or unconsciously – to heal the energy of our earlier choices. This is how we progress at the soul level.

Why is it ever acceptable to kidnap, sell or kill another human being? Or any wonderful sentient being, whether it's an elephant, lion, gorilla, dolphin, whale, dog or cat?

How do we heal this energy NOW?

What is it going to take for us to live lives of peace and love, despite external events? To BE peace and love. It's why Lightworkers chose to be on Earth – to bring Light to what many consider a dark time.

It's our amazing planet's best hope for salvation. My Future Self Gwen incarnated to help restore the Heaven on Earth energy that is a critical component of the Divine Feminine, and specifically part of the Mary Magdalen energy.

I believe this is the reason so many women – and some men – are remembering their past lives as Mary Magdalen in the Yeshua ben Joseph/ Jesus timeline.

I don't see that timeline as being about religion or about the Bible, written by committee hundreds of years later. I see it as a historic timeline about an amazing healer and Christ's message that God is love.

***

On August 12th, 1676, Philip and his forces were surrounded in a swamp named Mount Hope. A Pocasset Native by the name of Alderman shot and killed Philip.

King Philip, formerly Metacomet, was quartered and beheaded for high treason according to the laws of the time in England.

The troops returned to Plimoth with the news that Philip – the English archenemy – was dead. The men were paid four shillings, sixpence each.

Philip was left unburied both as an example and because he had caused so many Englishmen not to be buried. His lifeless body was hung upon four trees.

His head was carried through the streets of Plimoth on August 17th, 1676, and then set upon a pole where it remained for nearly a quarter of a century.

I took great care never to look at poor Philip's head closely when I was in Plimoth after my death. It was too heartbreaking and disrespectful for me to bear.

I tried to send healing to the region, Natives and Colonial settlers alike. I should have first returned Home to heal my own tremendous emotions from my life at Plimoth Plantation.

***

Instead, I allowed my heartbreak to continually build for hundreds of years, compounding having seen Yeshua killed in the most brutal, humiliating way possible.

I had also seen my rollicking German husband Klaus Stortebeker and all our men – my dearest friends who had become family – beheaded in the Hamburg public square in 1401.

Our 'crime' as the Robin Hood Pirates was smuggling affordable food to the people through the corrupt government barricades.

I'd do it again in a heartbeat and so would Lance, who was my husband Klaus. I'm so grateful that we could have that conversation in present day.

Our life as that North Seas Pirate King and Queen is my favorite past life of the more than eighty I've consciously recalled.

***

Back in 1676, King Philip's War was essentially over. Final confrontations continued for several more months. Philip had never wavered from his determination of war to the death as he was fighting for his people's way of life.

Philip knew there would be no mercy for him, especially once his cherished wife and young son were captured and sold into slavery.

The Sachem Native leader Canonchet was also firm in his decision to fight to the death. Neither he nor Philip wanted such peace as we English would grant on what had been the Indians homeland for thousands of years.

We had simply outbred the Natives, with the Warren family leading the way. European disease caused the Indians more misery and cost them more lives than King Philip's War as they had no immunity for it.

***

Contrast this to the Natives generosity in accepting my presence as a ghost after my death. I was so confused by my sudden violent and unexpected death, and increasingly lonely over time because of my flawed decision to not travel Home without William.

William had said, 'I'll be back for you, Ann. Wait for me.'

I loved William. I believed in him. Therefore, I waited. And waited some more.

Somehow more than three hundred years passed.

The Native's kindness and humanity toward me was both generous and deeply appreciated. Many Natives chose to stay behind as ghosts after their deaths to work to heal the land and problematic energy of the region.

I'm unclear why they didn't choose to return Home first and return as Spirits? All I can conclude is we always have free will and learn from every choice we make.

The Native men graciously allowed me to stay with them. They were nothing but kind and respectful with me during my long stint as a ghost, like they were during my many years trading with them in our small trading post.

I was the only Englishwoman I'm aware of doing this work. There were few, if any Native women who volunteered for the difficult job to heal the land and energy of the region.

Perhaps the Native men saw me at a soul level and knew the Colonial Englishwoman life was only a blip in a soul's long journey. Conceivably they knew I understood and honored their way of life as I had many Native past lives of my own.

***

In 2014, Gwen unconsciously continued her work to send healing to the thousands who were at Plimoth.

If she had aligned with Spirit more skillfully and done so from 5D – the place of Unity Consciousness only – rather than from 4D Mass Consciousness, she would not have required healing herself from her spiritual teacher when she wore out her own aura.

The moment Gwen set foot at Plimoth Planation in 2014, she found several male Wampanoag lives of her own. They included having been captured and sent to England as a slave on a supply ship in the 'tween deck cargo hold.

No wonder she has such vivid memories of crossing the Atlantic on those grueling passages, having done so from various perspectives.

Her next incarnation was at Salem during the Witchcraft Trials. This is likely why she felt such an urge to move to Boston when she graduated from college as she had so much past life energy in that area to resolve. But she needed to wake up spiritually first, and that would take another twenty-five years.

***

I return now to my commentary regarding the end of the Colonial era. In 1681, Plimoth Colony Governor Thomas Hinckley negotiated for a royal charter.

On December 20th, 1686, Sir Edmund Andros arrived as governor of the Dominion of New England, politically combining the New York and New England colonies.

On April 22nd, 1688, Plimoth rose against Andros when word reached us of the accession of William and Mary to England's throne.

Thomas Hinckley resumed his governorship. On October 7th, 1691, England combined the Plimoth and Maine colonies with Massachusetts Bay.

On May 14th, 1692, Sir William Phips arrived in Boston with the new charter. June 8th, 1692 was the last meeting of the Plimoth General Court.

The Colonial era was officially over, though many historians include the Salem Witchcraft Trials of 1693 as being part of the Colonial period, as do I.

My soul developed serious energetic issues from not going Home to heal after my lifetime as Ann Warren Little. I eventually became 'The Broken-Hearted Ghost' that Gwen first encountered as a newlywed in 1989.

I was so despondent I was no longer interested in returning Home. I took a lot of convincing as I was also ridiculously stubborn. I'd been strong for so long simply to survive but took a strength too far and became incredibly willful.

I had forgotten to align with Divine Will – God's Will. I had forgotten the power of Divine Right Timing. I had forgotten the beauty of aligning with 'The Flow' of the Universe, which is why my Guides asked me to use 'The Flow' as the book title for this series.

I finally went Home in 2013 with the help of multiple healers and caring, patient friends. The Mystic Robin Alexis played a tremendous part in my healing during the years 2013-2017. I am extremely grateful to her as she changed my life in so many positive ways.

***

I would like to publicly thank Lance as it was a generous and *much needed act on his part to help Gwen get me – Anna Warren Little's ghost – Home in 2013.*

Lance and Gwen had broken up eighteen months earlier when she told him the incredibly complex story she had been piecing together regarding Plimoth. When she asked for his help to send her own ghost from the 1600s Home, he listened intently for over an hour, interrupting only with a few clarifying questions.

Lance's response to Gwen's long narrative regarding what went wrong between them at Plimoth Plantation was simple:

'I believe you. How can I help you make this right? We need to fix this now.'

What a superb example of holding space for someone to allow them to do their own healing work! With Lance's help, I was able to do a soul retrieval of my energy as Ann Warren Little. I could then begin to finally heal my heartbreak, raise my vibration and become sovereign in my own energy.

My physical and emotional health improved markedly over the next few years once my ghost was Home. I was no longer constantly battling with low vibration energy getting into my field, which caused tremendous physical and emotional pain, confusion, and excessive emotion.

I learned how to ground and clear my energy, and to fully align with my Higher Self and Spirit Guides. I began to teach others to do the same.

Chapter 10

I lived at the New Colony from when I was a twelve-year-old girl until my death as a widow in my sixties.

I spent over three hundred years digesting my Plimoth Plantation experiences.

My Guides tell me I still had thirty percent energy as a disincarnated entity, or ghost. It surprises me my energy remained that high for such a long period of time.

It appears I stored up a great wealth of information from the 1600s as well as from certain earlier lives to help clear the past life energy not only for myself but for mankind.

**

My Higher Self fully expected my 1800s Future Self Gretchen Elliott to get Ann Warren Little's ghost Home.

I specifically scripted a happy, peaceful 'rest life' as a childless female writer in remote Othello, in what is now Washington State.

I feel I married the soul who had been Captain William Pierce that life to help me get Ann Home. But I didn't sufficiently wake up spiritually as Gretchen, which likely led to our contract for him to wake me up spiritually in my current life as Gwen.

I wrote approximately fifty novels as Gretchen Elliott but was not published. My books were all lost as we had no children to leave them to.

My husband John Elliott (now Lance) was also a writer during our gentleman farmer life in Othello, as was our mutual friend Didi. Didi was a male that lifetime, and her (his) life partner Preston was an author, too.

Didi heard 'John Elliott' was Gwen's husband's name during a hypnotherapy session when Didi was the client.

John Elliott is also Gwen's grandfather's name in her current incarnation.

But Didi didn't know Gwen's grandfather's name this lifetime – she simply heard it as validation for Gwen that they had indeed found another of their shared past lives.

Gwen's husband's name was one of several interesting synchronicities, as was the tiny town's name Othello. The name Preston would also become a helpful marker.

When Gwen was driving home after spending the day looking for potential past life clues in Othello, Lance took an unexpected nap while she drove. This freed Gwen to converse with her Guides. She asked her Spirit Guides to show her a sign if she had indeed had a past life in Othello as a female writer married to Lance.

In less than a minute, she heard an excited "Look, look!" from her Guides. She glanced around the small rural highway sharply to ensure there was no collision to avoid.

She saw the next exit was for the town of Preston. Preston was Didi's partner that life, and Gwen's friend. What were the odds? It was an unusual first name, especially for a woman, and likely was originally a family surname.

She heard a quiet 'Past life confirmed.'

I feel my husband John Elliott was published that lifetime, and possibly Didi. I would love to find their books but haven't been able to locate them so far as I don't know the book titles or exact year of publication.

Gwen will tell the story of the 'Two Writing Couples' more fully in a future book, including how that lifetime in rural Othello, Washington tied back to her Shakespeare life, as Shakespeare wrote 'Othello.'

***

I return now from Othello to my life at Plimoth. I feel a major piece of what went wrong in Colonial America was Puritan self-righteousness taken too far.

I've learned the hard way that strengths become weaknesses when they become excessive, like great strength becoming stubbornness and inflexibility.

This merciless, self-righteous energy would culminate in the dreadful Salem Witchcraft Trials of 1692 to 1693.

Salem is located sixty-four miles north of Plimoth. Both are waterfront towns with Salem about a half-hour north of Boston and Plimoth an hour south.

Some Puritans used the Bible – especially the books of the Old Testament – to harden themselves to mercy.

Salem became a notorious mass hysteria and a horrifying lack of due process under the law. More than two hundred people in Salem were accused of witchcraft. Witch hysteria also broke out in nearby Andover and Ipswich.

Religious intolerance, fear and ignorance once again made for a powder keg – had we learned nothing from the religious intolerance that led to our leaving England for first Holland and then the New World in 1620?

Many stood trial. About twenty were hanged or pressed to death by stones being laid upon their chests. This causes suffocation, as does crucifixion.

Some victims were water-tortured. Some died of starvation and exposure in the jail cells, and some thankfully escaped.

I testified at Salem as a teenaged girl to help end the Witchcraft Trials during my next life after Plimoth. It was terrifying to speak up, as one could then quickly become accused of witchcraft themselves.

The stakes were especially frightening for me as I've had a lot of energy to release from multiple lives as both a white witch and one practicing the dark arts.

It's important to remember we've all been 'Saints and Sinners' and to not judge others as it's not our job.

Thank you for listening to my story as Ann Warren Little of Plimoth Plantation. It is an immense gift to truly hear and see another, regardless if that soul is incarnated or a ghost.

We all crave human connection, including to feel loved, respected, appreciated and understood.

***

It was a tremendous turning point for Gwen when Lance told her, 'I believe you,' when she shared with him what was occurring with her unbalanced ghost energy from the 1600s and what his part in it was, from her perspective.

I finally returned Home as Ann Warren Little in stages, after hundreds of years.

- *Gwen and Lance held a ceremony at his house in the spring of 2013 to help me get Home. I finally felt heard and vindicated. This was a tremendous step and vital to my being able to journey back to the Light.*

- *I thank them for their leap of faith in doing a ceremony at first for me and then with me, though neither had any conscious memory of how to do a ritual. Both followed their hearts and had a pure intent to help make things right. That's all that's needed. Both Gwen and Lance were compassionate but firm with me like Abby had been the first night she tried to send me Home.*

- *A few days later Gwen worked with her spiritual teacher to incorporate me back into her timeline. This is called a soul retrieval and is most often done by a Shaman but can be done by other experienced healers. Some individuals can do their own soul retrievals with their Guides.*

- *I attended Lance's birthday party the next weekend as Gwen. I was finally publicly acknowledged by Lance as Captain William Pierce!*

- *Gwen sent me Home more fully on her own from her house that night as I had asked to attend William's birthday party first. It was surprisingly challenging. She shook like a leaf for much of the next day as there was so much energy to release and to upgrade. My Future Self heard to drink as much water as possible and managed to eat a few saltine crackers and a few bites of cheese and fruit. She was beyond exhausted yet could only sleep fitfully for less than an hour at a time as she midwifed the birth of her sovereign self.*

- *Gwen heard to burn white candles to symbolize White Light permeating her aura to replace the lower vibration energy leaving her field in droves.*

- *When releasing a lot of energy that no longer serves you, it's a best practice to replace it with higher vibration energy.*

- *You may need to repair any energy imprints or divets that remain. Ascended Master Mother Mary (Jesus' mother) is the specialist for this – anyone can call on her. This has nothing to do with religion – it's energy work, and we're all nothing but energy. Visualize pink healing light to help with the process.*

- *I then fully incorporated into Gwen's timeline and went Home a final time during her Quantum Healing Hypnotherapy (QHHT) session in late June of 2013.*

***

I'm deeply grateful to all involved. Ann Warren Little has clearly been a complex and critical soul retrieval for not only Gwen, but for my entire soul's journey.

Many individuals from my Plimoth Plantation life reincarnated with me again in my present life. This provided the opportunity for me to assemble the puzzle pieces of what occurred during my life, death and after-life as Ann Little in 1676. I'm truly thankful for their help.

I reiterate my belief our lives can best be thought of as plays that we carefully plan, cast and then act out to learn specific lessons including excellent boundaries and forgiveness.

We plan our curriculum before we return to Earth school once again, to use another analogy.

The purpose is to provide our souls with the opportunity to progress. The soul craves experiences, above all else, as this is how we learn to become peace and love once again.

Gwen's 'Playbill' from the New Colony includes:

- My friend Abby that recognized I was a ghost. Abby was Ann's best friend, next-door neighbor and trading post co-worker.
- My youngest daughter Tanya was Ann's eldest sister Mary Warren.
- My mother Elizabeth was Ann's stepmother Elizabeth Walker Warren.
- My current father was once again Ann's father Richard Warren.
- My stepmother was Ann's mother who died from childbed fever in England.
- A Facebook friend in Canada was my younger brother Nathaniel.
- A former co-worker was my brother-in-law Robert Bartlett, married to my eldest sister Mary.
- My former husband was my 'spurned suitor.'
- My former lover Lance was Captain William Pierce.
- My cat Midnight was with me when I was a widow and during my death as Ann Little on the tiny front porch of my

home. He hid in my walk-in closet during my first Quantum Healing Hypnotherapy session. He had always tried to run out of our present-day house and then would stop on the front porch and look wildly around in all directions and be very agitated. I believe he was watching for an Indian attack as far-fetched as that may sound. Midnight has not done that once since our healing session as I believe he released the old energy and finally forgave himself for my death from when I went to let him inside but instead and died from an Indian arrow.

- A ruthless business competitor was Captain Myles Standish.

- A Facebook friend who lives just a few miles from the present-day Plimoth Plantation living museum was King Philip.

- I was to reunite with my past life husband Thomas Little as my new life partner. He was not capable of it energetically, so we did not meet beyond a thirty-second encounter in an elevator. I wish him well as I chose to move on after four years spent sending love and healing to my Twin-Flame, also known as the other half of my soul.

***

I wouldn't learn the details of William's death as Ann for more than three hundred years. Gwendolyn Rose explained to me what had happened to William with Lance by her side in the spring of 2013.

I recognized Lance immediately as Captain Pierce. I'd finally found William! That was the night Gwen and Lance first helped me begin to journey Home.

I'd been a ghost for so long I could no longer find my way to the Light. I needed help – I so needed more energy, clarity, love and compassion.

I hadn't known William had died a hero at sea when I was around thirty years of age when I was Ann. I had been married to Thomas for almost a decade. We had four beautiful daughters, with five more children yet to be born.

William died that lifetime at age forty-six. He died as he lived, much larger than life.

William's final voyage was to the Caribbean. He was relocating Colonists to Providence as the Ship's Master for the

Desire. She arrived at New Providence in the Bahamas on July 13th, 1641, moments after the Spanish had captured it.

William became suspicious he was sailing into a trap but there wasn't enough time to heave-to with his ship under full sail. I heard he gallantly faced his death.

The Spanish had so suddenly rained cannon fire down upon the Desire! Captain Pierce immediately sent all passengers and crewmen down into the hold for safety. He remained lying on deck with one sailor, the minimum necessary to sail his ship.

William lay in the caboose to watch the Desire's sails. He and the lone sailor above board were fatally wounded by the same wide load of cannon shot.

They were buried at sea. It's what William would have wanted.

I'm glad it feels like he had a few moments to make his peace with God. He did see his death coming when I tune into watching what happened so long ago. I trust he journeyed Home to God quickly and easily, unlike me.

***

Captain William Pierce played a vital role in settling America. Ship's Master Pierce once sailed the three thousand miles between England and New England in a record-setting twenty-three-day journey. That is still an impressive feat over three hundred years later.

He became the most celebrated and traveled Sea Captain of our time, with over two-hundred and fifty successful voyages.

William Pierce was a God-fearing, highly intelligent and literate man. He published the first bound book in the English language in North America. Captain Pierce and his brother John were credited with helping set the spelling conventions that still have an impact today.

***

Gwen snickered in recognition when she learned about William's anger over the spelling mistakes made by the illiterate Boston printer who first published 'Pierce's Almanac.'

William is the author of the famous Pierce's Almanac which she had known about since grade school.

Lance is still as precise with language, spelling and grammar today. It was one of the many synchronicities shown to her that Lance had been Captain William Pierce.

No one else would include in his Match dating profile that he was 'only interested in meeting a woman with excellent verbal and written communication skills, including correct grammar and spelling.'

How fitting he then met Gwen, with her many writer past lives, including one married to him when they were both full-time writers in tiny Othello, Washington.

Lance still has that same crackling 'larger than life' energy today. And he still looks and walks like a Sea Captain as well as a Pirate.

Chapter 11

My maternal grandfather told me privately several times when I was in high school and again during college to 'Always remember we came over on the Mayflower ships!'

Was he referring to our ancestors or to us quite literally in our future lifetimes? I was never sure what to make of it until I fully understood that our souls are eternal and incarnate many times.

My grandfather wasn't a fanciful man – he lived through the Great Depression and had always worked hard to support and take care of his family. We never discussed the possibility of reincarnation and past lives.

I thought in the late 1970s and early 1980s he was mistaken in referring to the Mayflower ships in the plural, but he was correct. In 2013 I found his name on the Ship's Rolls from the Colonial era while searching for my own identity at Plimoth. I believe my grandfather incarnated and went to Virginia in the 1600s while I went to Plimoth.

He then used the same first and last name from the Colonial era when he incarnated as my mother's father in 1906. He was born on Chincoteague Island, Virginia, only about 150 miles from Jamestown. Lots of synchronicities.

This helped me solve the mystery of my past life in Colonial America. My grandfather called me 'Annie' each time he told me about my Mayflower ship heritage. I thought he was simply getting older and mistakenly using my mother's childhood nickname instead of my name.

But the memory of his calling me 'Annie' as he spoke about our Mayflower ship heritage remained with me for more than thirty years to help me finally solve the puzzle.

I was having dinner with my former boyfriend Lance. We kept reuniting in remarkable ways as we hadn't yet completed our lessons together. Pay attention if this happens to you and ask *the lesson to be able to move through it more quickly and gracefully.*

I didn't fully appreciate what my grandfather had told me as a high-school aged Gwen until 2013. That was when I began to experience an even more profound and rapid spiritual awakening. He reminded me of it all so patiently from the other side of the Veil.

My grandfather showed me the scene of us talking out on the enclosed porch of my grandparents Florida retirement home decades earlier. Additional memories from my past lives began to flood in as I had dinner that night with Lance.

My maternal grandfather was my primary Spirit Guide for a time. He showed me my life as Ann Warren Little at Plimoth Plantation that evening, though I didn't know my name at first.

My grandfather had passed away in the mid-1990s yet I could suddenly hear him as clear as day? It was a profound unexpected opening of my psychic clairs especially my clairaudience (the ability to hear Spirit), and my other clairs to a lesser degree.

I was flabbergasted to have a spontaneous recall of my past life at Plimoth while having dinner in a Seattle-area Mexican restaurant with a friend. I didn't consider myself psychic at the time and didn't appreciate how rapidly my Past Life Reader abilities were beginning to blossom as they were needed to fulfill my life purpose and larger soul mission.

That night at dinner Lance mentioned one of his lives where he had died at sea. He was unable to return to a woman who was waiting for him. He said she had not been able to release her anger with him as she didn't know what had occurred and didn't get the closure she needed.

I gaped at him. Time stood still for a moment, and then reorganized itself cohesively into 'another time, another place, one that will have the best healing and information for your life today,' as I now suggest to my clients during their *Regression Healing/ Past-Life Regression sessions.*

Lance's comment about his life as a Sea Captain triggered me to remember my life at Plimoth Plantation like a bolt from the blue! I gaped at him across the table. I knew who he'd been before in my life.

Lance was the Sea Captain I had loved with all my heart and waited for so long. He was the Captain who brought me with my family to the New Colony in the 1600s.

This was the man I'd dreamed about so many times. This was the man I'd been waiting for on my property in Massachusetts both back when I first married in this life and several hundred years earlier!

This HAD to be the key to help the heartbroken ghost... the ghost who was me.

***

We spoke animatedly until midnight in that Mexican restaurant. We were also resolving our past life at Camelot.

We were so focused, and the healing energy was flowing so strongly I never noticed the restaurant staff pile the chairs on the tables all around us, wash the floors and prepare to close the restaurant for the night.

The staff were so kind not to interrupt us. I would not have noticed a bomb go off during those several hours while the comprehensive memories from both Plimoth Plantation and Camelot poured in with astounding clarity.

I scribbled notes and questions furiously on a full-size legal pad I fortuitously had with me. Lance helped me organize my thoughts and the materials for what would become a key portion of this trilogy.

He had been a reporter and was a writer. Lance was the perfect person to help me begin to outline both lives on paper, as well as list our numerous questions. There were so many missing pieces as this energy was both immensely complex and surreal to try to absorb.

It took me several weeks of focused daily work with my Spirit Guides to piece together my identity as Ann Warren Little and Lance's as Captain William Pierce.

I didn't know our names at first, but I could feel into who we had been. I knew I needed to solve the mystery of my sad *and confused ghost to finally find peace for her and for myself both in my current life and as an eternal soul.*

I realized over the next few years that about a dozen people in my current life were also with me at Plimoth.

Several have remarkably similar names in the two lifetimes. These were some of the clues and synchronicities shown to me by Spirit that I was on the right track as a spiritual sleuth.

***

These identifications were aided greatly by meeting intuitive artist and metaphysical author Laurie Regan.

Within moments of our initial meeting and without mentioning I was struggling to heal and release my Colonial America life, Laurie drew me as a ghostly Ann Warren.

Laurie also gave me a highly accurate mini-reading that helped me release that lifetime. I was stunned and beyond grateful as I felt the invisible chains of the heavy energy from that life finally begin to lift.

Seeing my face as Ann helped me heal and release that past life where I had become literally stuck as Earth-bound energy.

I recognized immediately I was looking at the same heartbroken ghost I had seen so many times on my property in Boxford, Massachusetts back when I was a newlywed. And she was me!

***

Next, Laurie drew a sketch from Spirit while at home alone a day or two after we met. She didn't recognize who the woman was that she had just drawn. Laurie shared her pencil drawing on her Facebook page, hoping someone might recognize the young woman.

I was flabbergasted to recognize Abby, my best friend from Plimoth when I signed on to Facebook later that day. Laurie's sketch immediately come up in my feed.

I immediately texted a screen shot of Laurie's drawing to Abby. I asked her simply if the sketch reminded her of anyone.

I didn't mention it was a past life sketch, how I had come into possession of it, nor anything about Laurie and her *unique abilities as an intuitive artist and writer.*

Abby texted me back immediately, 'That's me! How in the world did you get a sketch of me from the 1600s? This is wild.'

I didn't yet understand Laurie's gift doesn't require her to be sitting with someone to draw them in a past life. Laurie Regan draws directly from Spirit to help mankind. She is one of the few people I know with this ability.

The power of her sketches and other intuitive art is the energy they help release. The sketches can be simple drawings particularly if Laurie is working at an event and needs to produce them quickly.

Visit Laurie at https://www.facebook.com/laurie.belle.5 on Facebook or search etsy.com for LaurieReganCreations shop to view examples. Perhaps you'll find someone you recognize, or even one of your own past lives or Spirit Guides.

Visit Laurie's Facebook page at https://www.facebook.com/laurie.belle.5 or search etsy.com for LaurieReganCreations shop to view examples. Perhaps you'll find someone you recognize, or even one of your own past lives or Spirit Guides.

***

Forty-eight hours later Laurie drew a man she didn't recognize. She again posted the sketch on Facebook.

Laurie's Guides asked her to only give the drawing to the person who could solve the clue as to who 'Wayne' was to the man drawn – what was the relationship?

Laurie was told by Spirit the man she drew was well-known. Many might recognize him and ask for the sketch. The drawing was to go to the person who knew who Wayne was, as it was to help that person heal.

Laurie did not recognize she had drawn Ship's Master William Pierce. She did not know who Captain Pierce was historically.

At that point I was still struggling mightily to heal and release my past life as Ann Warren. I closed my eyes after again finding a sketch on Laurie's Facebook page that I recognized.

I asked my Guides who Wayne was to William Pierce. I heard telepathically that Wayne was William Pierce's brother and was also a Ship's Master.

Laurie confirmed the identification was exactly right, and I asked to buy the sketch. She carefully wrapped and mailed it to me, and I gave it to Lance for his birthday a few weeks later.

Lance is the spitting image of William Pierce in the 1600s. It's an excellent drawing, especially considering Laurie had not yet met Lance – it's simply not necessary as what's occurring is an energy release and healing.

***

I showed my cell phone photo of Captain Piece's sketch to a half dozen friends over the next few weeks. (At that time Lance and I had a lot of friends in common.)

I privately asked each person the same simple question: 'Does this drawing remind you of anyone?'

Every person replied without hesitation something along the lines of: 'Wow, that's a great sketch of Lance. Who drew it? It really captures him so well.'

It was hard to express that it was a past life sketch drawn by an intuitive artist who had never met him. I was struggling with my world view changing so quickly and dramatically.

My belief system was shifting so rapidly during parts of 2012-2014 that for a time I struggled to hold on to reality.

I felt like I had spiritual whiplash at times - I felt too untethered, too in-between worlds. I struggled with vertigo and a host of other physical ascension symptoms.

I did not yet know how to meaningfully ground or to center my own energy, which is vital, as is clearing and protecting one's energy and raising our vibration.

***

I showed the past life sketch of Ann Warren to Lance. I simply asked if he recognized her and once again gave no explanation.

He replied without hesitation, 'My God, that's you, a long time ago. I remember that sweet face so well!'

Lance paused. 'When was that?'

All I could do was nod at first as it was hard to speak past the lump in my throat. I sensed this was a tremendous breakthrough for us both, though I didn't yet fully understand what was happening, how or why.

I finally was able to reply I agreed it was a sketch of me from Colonial America. His face lit up with recognition.

I showed Lance the pencil sketch of my best friend Abby from Plimoth and asked him, 'Do you know who this is?'

He identified her on the spot with her full current name, and remarked she still has the same stunning bright blue eyes as she did back then.

Yet the sketch was drawn in graphite pencil. It had no color, yet he could somehow clairvoyantly see Abby's blue eyes? Lance is more psychic than he knows.

I could also see various colors in some of Laurie's pencil sketches back before she began adding color to them. I asked her how this could occur. She told me some people could see the colors energetically, though she hadn't physically drawn them.

***

The final surprise in that incredible, life-changing week was the fourth past life sketch from my time at Plimoth Plantation.

The sketch again appeared on Laurie's Facebook page with her asking if anyone recognized the man? Once again, the man felt very familiar to me. I felt chills all down my back and my Guides trying to get my attention, just like with the other three drawings.

The final Plimoth sketch was of a bearded male Pilgrim, recognizable by his clothing. The sketch came to Laurie with a single-word clue: 'Father.'

It took me a few days to identify him. I knew he wasn't my father Richard Warren.

Neither Abby or Lance recognized him from the sketch as we were now working these clues together, as all three of us felt we'd been at the New Colony together.

That seemed to imply only I knew the bearded Pilgrim. That narrowed the field considerably as Abby knew almost everyone I knew as we had spent a lifetime together at the New Colony, and there were only a few hundred people there. We knew essentially everyone.

Was 'Father' a title used in that time, like the term Mistress or Goodwife? I researched that possibility with the excellent Plimoth Plantation website. No, that didn't seem to fit either.

I finally got it during meditation as I continued to ask who Laurie had sketched in the Colonial outfit. One day I clearly heard 'The father of your children!'

I immediately saw the faces of my present life daughters. I asked if there was anything else to know about the man and heard 'Your spurned suitor.' Bingo!

I shared that info with Laurie. She confirmed she was hearing 'spurned suitor,' too, but didn't know what that term meant until we worked the puzzle together. It's an old-fashioned term neither of us use today.

Laurie told me she saw that earnest suitor enjoying a buggy ride with me when I was Ann. We were traveling along a small road that went past long rows of corn – acres and acres of tall, healthy stalks of corn.

Corn was a staple of our life at Plimoth. Laurie hadn't known that we grew corn there, and I verified her impression.

My spurned suitor's name at Plimoth was John Totman. It was amazing to recognize his name on-line on the Mayflower Ship's Rolls.

My former husband's name is remarkably similar. We were together for eighteen years. I'd like to publicly thank Jake for our marriage and our two beautiful daughters.

Our soul contract was to 'have a long marriage that we would both grow from, and to have beautiful children together,' as mentioned earlier. Contract fulfilled.

Neither Abby or William ever met my suitor as we only met the one time for a single carriage ride. This explained why I recognized the man in the sketch and they did not. The sketch looks a lot like my ex-husband does today, and again, Laurie never met him, saw a photo of him nor did I describe him in any way.

I highly recommend Laurie Regan's intuitive art as well as her metaphysical fiction, available on Amazon.

I am thrilled Laurie and I re-met, as we have traveled together before in other lives. I'm happy we are friends once again, as well as writing partners. I greatly appreciate Laurie's service to the planet.

Chapter 12

While it's subject to debate if we can or should change the past, we certainly can learn from other time periods and realities and powerfully reframe them to progress. We can heal and release pain and other emotions and energies that no longer serve us.

My belief is we can go back in time – or travel to a parallel time or space in another dimension – and visualize a happier, healthier outcome to improve our current reality.

We can request a change in a soul mate designation that no longer serves us. We can end or renegotiate soul contracts that do not help us in our current lives.

We can remove karmic cords on our own, or with assistance, once the lessons are learned. Archangel Michael specializes in removing cords. Anyone can request his amazing assistance.

Cutting karmic cords does not imply you will never meet again. I hear a lot of people hesitating to cut cords as they want to meet that individual again in a happier circumstance.

In my experience you will raise your vibration with your choice to master lessons and cut the cords as cords by their nature are low vibration.

My belief is we should all be sovereign in our own unique, beautiful energy. This can be a journey. It certainly was for me.

***

My belief is karma is a teaching tool, not punishment. It's a common misconception to blame one's 'bad karma' when things don't go the way we want. Ownership and a true desire to embrace one's lessons are all that's needed to transmute the karmic cords of attachment.

Not everyone has karma. My Guides tell me we need to transmute any karma to raise our vibration to 5D (the fifth spiritual dimension) and higher, along with aligning with our Higher Self and fully opening our Kundalini life force energy. This can be done safely via Kundalini yoga or meditation, for example.

My belief is it's crucial to ground our energy before ascending or we can become ungrounded, confused and out-of-touch with our current reality.

We can choose to end soul contracts that no longer serve us. We can improve our lives by addressing our past hurts as this will heal our souls where the eternal memory is stored. Emotions are timeless and need to be balanced, along with our left brains, more commonly known as the ego.

***

A vital part of our Higher Self is always at Home. When in a body I've learned to ground daily to the magnetic core of Mother Earth to find my best support and strength.

I find it beneficial to invite my Higher Self down into my body twice a day, morning and night, to be fully aligned.

Being grounded and clear in our energy allows us to fully 'be here now' and to embrace the moment. This is how we live the 'Heaven on Earth' energy of peace, love and joy.

We chose to come to Earth to have a body and to have experiences, though some of our experiences will likely confound us in the moment.

***

My personal belief is *all* souls should go to the Light once they drop their body. Though we have free will as to when and how we will return Home, Earth-bound energy may need your help. If you are comfortable helping a ghost journey Home, here are some techniques.

Ground and center your own energy first.

Let them know firmly but kindly they no longer have a body, and need to go Home to heal, and to be happy and free. They can return later for visits once they've raised their vibration.

You can tell the stuck soul about the amazing party and reunions they will experience at Home, and that it is the place of perfect love and peace, with no judgment. Explain that they deserve to be with the Light, and to release any shame or anger.

You can call on Mother/ Father God, the Angels or Guides including Ancestors or animals to assist a ghost or stuck soul. Just listen to your intuition as to what the ghost most needs.

You can help a ghost visualize floating up over the trees to the Light or taking a long staircase, escalator or tunnel up and up and up until they cross over. Let them know to tune into the flow of the Universe to find their way Home. They will be assisted, if necessary, and will often feel a magnetic tug to help them cross over.

You may invite the disincarnated energy to simply place their hand over their heart, and you do the same. Ask them to tune into feelings of love, peace and gratitude to float up to Home in their pure soul state.

They can shed their body, release any regrets and just go when it's their turn to heal and celebrate at Home!

If you're comfortable doing so, you can offer to take their hand and go part-way Home with them. Have strong boundaries and watch over your own energy and space with a compassionate heart so that your energy remains sovereign.

You may also be guided to simply speak with a ghost that you see or sense, sing or pray for them, clap your hands, drum, ring a bell, use a singing bowl, light some white candles, burn some sage or using your breath to provide them with some loving energy to move to the Light. This simple actions and rituals can provide them with the energy they need to return to the Light.

I trust I will never lose my way Home again.

Anna Warren Little
September 21, 2018 (International Day of Peace)

THE END

Epilogue

My process in working with past-life energy will likely make many reincarnation researchers groan with despair.

I'm aware many purist researchers question the accuracy of memories from past-life regression hypnotherapy sessions.

That feels like a bias to me, and not one that I fully understand.

My focus is to resolve pain and other energy that no longer serves me, and to help others do the same to enjoy a better life. My 'proof' of a past life is does the person's life improve after releasing the energy regardless if they experienced memories from the collective, have a few details wrong, experienced a fantasy or were quite accurate with many of their memories. The word proof is used quite differently by reincarnation researchers.

I believe there's room for many approaches in the exciting field of reincarnation and past lives as well as in the related areas of NDEs (Near-Death Experiences), after-life research and the exploration of the survival of consciousness after the physical death of the human body.

I find the Police Captain Robert Snow, James Leininger and Christian Haupt/ Cathy Byrd reincarnation cases especially fascinating. You can look for them on-line.

Cathy Byrd's award-winning book, 'The Boy Who Knew Too Much' is currently being made into a film as it's such an intriguing case.

I'm certain it took a lot of courage for Cathy to publicly share her son Christian's memories of being 'a tall baseball player' in a previous life. Welcome back, Christina and Lou Gehrig – mother and son, once again.

It took me several years to understand why such extensive Plimoth Plantation memories came through in my current life.

I didn't realize at first that I was working to heal the Colonial experience at Plimoth not only for myself, but for other Colonials and Natives from that timeline, too.

I had to assemble the puzzle pieces slowly, as the jigsaw was so incredibly large and confusing when I began, particularly as my memories kept jumping timelines.

I was surprised when this story became best expressed as historical fiction in addition to metaphysical fiction, specifically a ghost story.

I spent much time in prayer and meditation to understand my lifetime as Ann Little at Plimoth. I used muscle-testing and my psychic clairs extensively during the years it took me to write what became a trilogy with a prequel.

I wrote over thirteen hundred pages in the first draft of 'The Flow' trilogy before this prequel came through originally as an epilogue.

I was triggered back so suddenly into my past life as Ann Warren when I saw the first few seconds of the commercial for National Geographic's 'Saints & Strangers' mini-series.

I was immediately pitching up and down aboard the Anne of London again, and felt old heartbreak that no longer serves me. I wisely went to bed early, asked for help from my Guides, and felt better by morning.

I asked my Guides why this occurred. I was asked to make every effort to complete 'The Flow' trilogy to help balance excessive emotion, including heartbreak, and to master forgiveness. Forgiveness is also the focus of my first non-fiction book, 'Regression Healing I: The Huntsman, the Lord High Mayor and the World Ward II Solider,' available from Amazon in paperback and Kindle formats and on Audible as an audio book.

I was shown how to reshape the lengthy epilogue into this prequel to set the stage for a metaphysical fiction trilogy inspired by my past lives. I've fictionalized some events for several reasons.

'The Flow I: Plimoth Plantation' (the novel) continues the story of Gwen's rapid spiritual awakening in the years 2010 to

2014. It completes the recounting of her Colonial America experience as Richard and Elizabeth Warren's second eldest daughter.

The 'The Flow II: The Divine Feminine,' contains many more of the approximately eighty past lives I've found since the first two were explored during a formal past-life regression in 2011.

'The Flow III: Mary Magdalen Remembers' focuses on Mary Magdalen and Yeshua ben Joseph's timeline, including Mary Magdalen's ten years training at the Egyptian Temple of Isis at Philae.

***

The question has arisen many times what did Ann do during the several hundred years she chose to remain Earth-bound as a ghost?

My distinct memories are three-fold:

1. Waiting and watching for William to return, so I could go Home.

2. Working with the Wampanoag to heal the land from King Philip's War. This somehow involved travel from Plimothn Planation (Massachusetts) to Telos – a city from the lost continent of Lemuria – via Middle Earth.

   My personal belief is Telos is now located within Mt. Shasta, California as the Heart-Center of the Universe; and

3. Participating in family life, to the best of my ability – attending special occasions such as holidays, birthdays, weddings, christenings, funerals, and more.

***

I stored all these memories from my life as Ann Warren Little in the Akashic Records – the storehouse of all knowledge – to share with a Future Self. I chose Gwendolyn Rose as she best heard and understood me, over time, once she released her fear.

Bless you for reading or listening to the narration of my life story in England, at Plimoth Plantation, and finally as a ghost.

Much healing can occur when we truly feel heard. It's a gift we can give freely to others. It's about simply being there and holding space with quiet strength and no judgment. Holding space does not imply you can or should fix the challenges for your loved one – instead, trust them to do their own work and empower them to find their own best path.

"THE WOMAN WHO HAUNTED HERSELF"

I met a remarkable woman in early 2013 when I most needed her help. Divine Right Timing.

Donya Wicken and her partner Ben (who's on the other side) are experts at helping stuck souls – ghosts – get to the Light.

Donya and Ben helped me understand what I needed to do to get Ann Warren Little Home. With my consent, Donya wrote a fabulous summary of what occurred.

With Donya's permission, I am including it here.

Visit her website **TheZenofBen.com** for more adventures helping disincarnates return to Source:

http://www.thezenofben.com/the-woman-who-haunted-herself

The Woman Who Haunted Herself by Donya Wicken

'I suppose once you start wrapping your mind around ideas like non-local consciousness and reincarnation and non-linear time you can pretty much expect weird things to happen. Recently we got a request for help from a woman (I'll call her Judy) who was being haunted. Judy had a great deal of experience with mediums and hypnotherapy and past life regressions. She had learned about several of her past lives including one in Camelot and one in Colonial America.

Meanwhile Judy in the 21st century was involved in a relationship of the sort that is described on Facebook as "It's Complicated." In this case FB should probably provide an option for "It's Very Very Complicated." One of the complicating factors is that, with the help of her team of paranormal experts, Judy learned that (we'll call him) Tony is her "primary soul mate." Now Ben and others have explained that being soul mates does not make two people good romantic partners or candidates for marriage. In fact, usually it portends just the opposite. It could mean that this person is in your life for the purpose of making you so miserable you will be forced to learn an unpleasant lesson.

What makes this relationship even more complicated is that Tony is the reincarnation of Captain Elijah Farthing, captain of the ship that had brought the earlier incarnation of Judy and her family to the new world. He was also the man the young Colonial Judy fell in love with, not knowing he was already married.

Evidently Captain Elijah died when his time came and crossed over and eventually reincarnated as Tony who intermittently loved Judy but not just Judy. Tony was something of a rogue. But Judy refused to give up on him.

Meanwhile, back in the colonies Judy, who for our purposes was then named Ruth, was killed by an arrow during war between the white settlers and the local native Americans. She left her body quickly but then refused to cross over and join her loved ones on the Other Side. For reasons best known to herself, she opted to stay and help the Indian spirits protect the land. When her loved ones on the Other Side tried to encourage her to come home she refused. She said she was waiting for Captain Elijah. She waited for over three hundred years.

Eventually Judy and Ruth met up because Ruth was haunting the land where she had lived in the 1600s which later Judy and her first husband purchased in the 1900s. It took the help of some psyche-savvy helpers to figure out what was going on but they finally informed Judy that the ghost was Ruth, her earlier incarnation. It seems Judy was haunting herself.

Donya was so bewildered by this story that she had to start referring to herself in the third person. For one thing in all the time she had been willing to think about reincarnation she assumed you had to cross-over and report to headquarters or something before you could reincarnate. Accounts of Lives Between Lives and even Ben's stories of The

Timeless Spaceless Place always suggest that souls go "home" before they embark on another incarnated adventure.

But evidently that is not always the case because there was Ruth becoming increasingly disruptive. She was also starting to demand attention from Tony whom she recognized as the man who, in her opinion, should have married her back in the colony.

Judy finally asked Ben what to do. While Donya may have been overwhelmed by the complexity of the stories and the amazing cast of characters, most of whom have been left out of this account, Ben was not. He listened to (read) the whole story and then stepped up and addressed Judy.

BEN: Judy, your ghost is you and you are your ghost. It's time for you to learn the lesson she didn't learn in her life time. If you want her to let go and move on you have to let go and move on. You are as stubborn as she is and she is as stubborn as you are. If you can't learn to let go you will have to come back and do it again and then there will be three of you. It's not going to stop until the lesson is learned. I understand about wanting to be with your soul mate. But that is part of what you need to learn. Someone being your soul mate doesn't make him what you want him to be. It sounds to me like his job this time is to break your heart until you stop letting him.

Judy wanted to know what she could do to get Ruth to go home. Ben pulled no punches.

BEN: You have to have a conversation with her and tell her that you will let go of the man who is breaking your heart and she must do the same. Assure her that in the Timeless Spaceless Place you will all have a glorious reunion and everything will be right. When you let go, Ruth will let go.

There's no point in sprinkling holy water around or burning incense. She's not doing anything inappropriate as far as she is concerned. Once she realizes that her soul has learned to put on her big girl panties she will do likewise and move on.

Judy was not offended by Ben's forthright speech and agreed to talk to Ruth. Tony and Judy talked to her together. Ruth agreed that it was time for her to leave but said she wanted to stay for Tony's upcoming birthday party. Tony and Judy (reluctantly) agreed.

It was the kind of "it's complicated" party that might be expected when ex-lovers and new lovers and literal ghosts from the past show up along with all sorts of other friends and relations. Stressful but actually fun in spite of everything.

At the party, instead of gifts, guests were encouraged to present roasts and toasts they had written. Judy announced that she wanted to read an anonymous note from someone who was not able to be physically present. Everyone wondered who the note was from except Tony. He told Judy to thank Ruth for him and to tell her that she had been very special to him.

It is often the case with spirits who refuse to cross that they are waiting for some sort of apology or acknowledgement from someone they love. Tony's words addressed to her in public seemed to satisfy Ruth's need to hear from Captain Elijah. She was now ready to move on.

Later Ruth reported that once she decided to move into the Light it was easy and her arrival was joyous. Judy still had a lot of healing and recovery to do but she felt that the way was clear now.

***

Hi. This is Ben. I'm Donya's Ghosty Friend. Sometimes she thinks the things that have happened to her since she met me are kind of crazy. But I tell her not to worry. People haunt themselves all the time without even being dead. It's a lot more interesting to be haunted by a self from three hundred years ago than one who just refuses to let go of a bad feeling or an unpleasant memory from last week. Be nice to yourself. And remember to always be nice to ghosts. The ghost you find in your closet could be YOU!

ABOUT THE AUTHOR

Wendy Rose Williams was born in Granby, Quebec, Canada. One of her fond childhood memories is falling asleep to the sound of lions roaring at the nearby Granby Zoo.

Wendy lived in Montreal, Florida, Atlanta, upstate New York and Boston before making her home in the Seattle area as of 1993. She has two daughters and a healing cat named Midnight.

Wendy enjoys being an active volunteer with the Dog Gone Seattle Rescue, though Midnight won't allow her to bring her 'work' home!

She has a profound understanding of past life energy as well as how to help people release pain and other energy that no longer serves them.

Wendy works with private clients as well as facilitates group workshops and is a frequent conference speaker. She enjoys speaking on a variety of spiritual topics on radio and recording her own publications as audio books.

TRAINING & CERTIFICATIONS

- Trained with Brian Weiss, MD (author 'Many Lives, Many Masters') Hypnotherapy and Past-Life Regression – 2018
- Life Between Lives Regression Therapy with Karen Wells (Karen was one of Dr. Michael Newton's original students and has been part of The Newton Institute training hypnotherapists around the world.) 2017-2018
- Certified Spiritual Teacher – 2017
- Mystic Radio Institute 'Evolutionary Foundations Levels I, II, and III' with Robin Alexis – 2016-2017
- Private Cosmic Coaching five-course series – 2016
- Reiki Levels I, II & III/ Reiki Master level training with Rus Sullivan (Edmonds, Washington) 2014 – 2016
- Channeling Levels 101, 102, 103 & 104 with Karen Downing (Issaquah, Washington) 2014 – 2016
- Certified as a Regression Healing Practitioner by Chris Turner, the Quantum Healing Centre
- (West Wellow, United Kingdom) 2014
- Ordained Minister, Universal Life Church
- (Modesto, California) 2014
- Master's in Business Administration 1984

AUTHOR CONTACT INFORMATION & COMPLIMENTARY PAST LIFE SKETCH OFFER

Website:WendyRoseWilliams.com
Facebook: facebook.com/gwendolyn.rose.79

Email Wendy@WendyRoseWilliams.com to request your complimentary copy of the Plimoth Plantation sketches described in this novel.

Wendy also has photos of the marker recognizing Thomas and Ann Little as original founders of the town of Marshfield, Massachusetts.

Your email address will be kept confidential and not sold or shared. You may receive occasional updates from the author including requests for test readers, and notifications of new publications, programs and workshops. You may opt-out at any time.

COMPLIMENTARY DISCOVERY SESSION OFFER

Visit WendyRoseWilliams.com to learn more about the benefits of a Regression Healing/ Past-Life Regression session.

Wendy offers private no-charge 30-minute Discovery Session phone appointments to explore whether you may wish to work together.

SNEAK PREVIEW OF
THE FLOW I:
PLIMOTH PLANTATION
(THE NOVEL)

*A METAPHYSICAL FICTION
TRILOGY BY*
WENDY ROSE WILLIAMS

Chapter 1: Uninvited Visitor

Gwen quietly pressed the 'End' button on her iPhone. She was stunned by what Abby Morehouse, her best friend of fifteen years, had just shared with her so delicately, and in precise detail – Gwen had a ghost!

Gwen was sitting comfortably on the carpeted floor of her master bedroom. Her back was propped against her queen-sized bed.

She stared at her bookcase and realized she was holding her breath. Gwen tried focusing on her breathing while she wrapped her mind around the unthinkable.

Abby had just provided Gwen with not only unasked-for verification of a ghost on her former property in Massachusetts, but the revelation that Gwen shared the same soul energy as that ghost. This implied that a part of her existed in limbo three thousand miles away.

Gwen heard the spine-chilling sound of a phonograph needle, scratching hard across a record. Her recollection of vinyl discs reminded her: Yes, she was that old. The humor of the situation was not lost on her.

***

Gwen was ready to end their conversation on an unrelated subject when Abby had asked her quietly, 'Do you have five more minutes?'

Gwen's intuition drummed rapidly.

'Get ready for a major curve ball,' she told herself. Her heart began pounding hard even before Abby began to launch into her narrative.

Gwen listened intently as Abby told her about having recently gone to East-West Bookshop, the largest metaphysical bookstore in Seattle.

Abby had planned to buy the newest Dr. Brian Weiss book regarding reincarnation and past lives. Yet once inside, Abby was inexplicably drawn repeatedly to a book entitled 'Sacred Spaces,' instead of the Weiss title she planned.

She bought 'Sacred Spaces' instead, feeling puzzled but honoring there was an unspoken urgency to her purchase.

When Abby arrived home, she set 'Sacred Spaces' down on the small built-in kitchen desk in the comfortable Seattle Eastside home she shared with her husband and children.

She tried walking away to catch up on a dozen things prior to her son and daughter's customary burst through the front door after school. But Abby was irresistibly drawn back to 'Sacred Spaces.'

She thumbed through it rapidly, still unclear why she had felt so compelled to buy it. Abby quickly found the section she was meant to read.

It concerned how to keep your home clear of ghosts or other low-vibration entities.

'What the heck?' she mused to herself.

Her home had no energy issues, and she cleared it regularly of any unwanted presences with sage and her conscious intent. Yet Abby read the section carefully how to clear a ghost before moving on with her busy daily routine.

She filed the odd experience away in the back of her mind. Abby was half-expecting it when she needed the 'Sacred Spaces' information a few days later.

***

She was awakened from a sound sleep just after midnight early in 2013. Her small dog Moonbeam was staring at her intently from the floor next to her side of the bed. The canine was quickly becoming agitated.

Abby reluctantly got up and stepped into her slippers and robe, wondering if her apparently nervous pet needed to be let out. She quietly walked the length of the house toward the kitchen with the dog racing ahead, trying not to wake her sleeping family.

Abby opened the sliding glass doors for Moonbeam. She hoped the dog would be quick with her doggy business in their fenced back yard, so she could get back to sleep.

Abby was startled when Moonbeam instead raced into their adjoining living room instead of going outside. Their small white dog began barking with all her might.

Abby could sense something up high to her right, at the very edge of her peripheral vision. What was that, up on the living room ceiling?

She turned and took a step down into her sunken living room. The petite brunette worked to quiet Moonbeam as her top priority.

Her son Adam's kitten suddenly joined the tense scene. The cat arched its back upon arrival, hissed madly, and raced back out of the living room.

***

Abby realized with an immediate knowing she was looking at a ghost. This was a specter from long ago, and shockingly, someone she knew. How could this be happening? And why?

The agitated shadow was swirling around rapidly on the living room ceiling in tight little circles. Abby felt deep heartbreak and pain emanating from the young female entity.

Abby knew immediately who the ghost was. It was Gwen from one of their shared past lives. A life they had only recently begun to discover.

She steeled herself not to give Gwen's ghost any signs of being welcome. Abby had to work hard not to be pulled into the immense heartbreak from one of her best friends – it was surprisingly touch and go.

She had learned from reading 'Sacred Spaces' that giving sympathy only prolongs the process of moving a ghost out of one's own home or sacred space.

Abby began talking firmly to the presence. Her intentions were kind.

'You don't have a body, you need to go Home!' Abby told the presence repeatedly.

Her inexplicable purchase of 'Sacred Spaces' suddenly made sense. She silently thanked Spirit for preparing her with the perfect tools.

It took a half-hour to get Gwen's ghost to leave. And Abby wasn't confident the ghost had gone to the Light...

(to be continued)

ALSO BY THE AUTHOR

'*Regression Healing I: The Huntsman, the Lord High Mayor and the World War II Soldier'* is the first in a series of client past-life regression sessions with Wendy Rose Williams. The non-fiction book is available in paperback and Kindle versions from Amazon.com.

'Regression Healing I' is also available on Audible.com as an audio book read by the author.

Autographed copies are available for purchase by U.S. residents directly from the author. Email Wendy@WendyRoseWilliams.com for more information.

SHORT STORIES

Wendy's first short story, 'A Tiny Bow and Arrow' won a writing contest. It was included in 'The Best of Spiritual Writers Network 2014: An Inspirational Collection of Short Stories and Poems.'

'*Ramona Falls: The Path to Forgiveness*'

Can Jesse Applegate, Oregon Wagon Train Leader, learn to forgive himself for the many deaths that occur along the trail in 1843?

'*The Car Whisperer: Trust Your Intuition*'

Gwen learns the hard way – and from a most unlikely teacher – to trust her intuition.

'*Jack's Journey Home*'

Can an elderly man suffering from a severe head injury truly have been one of the Apostles?

WORKS IN PROGRESS
NON-FICTION

Additional client sessions in the 'Regression Healing' series

- 'Regression Healing II: Joe & Marilyn'
- 'Regression Healing III: The Great Flood of 1889'
- 'Regression Healing IV: The Music in his Soul'

METAPHYSICAL FICTION NOVELS

'The Flow I: Plimoth Plantation' (the novel)

Gwendolyn Audrey Rose's prescription for on-line dating from her OB/GYN physician has startling results. She unintentionally manifests her primary and teaching soul mate only to discover they share more than a dozen past lives as well as significant challenging karma. Their romance doesn't work in this lifetime as she wants it to, but Gwen can't let it go. She learns the ghosts of our past can be startlingly real.

Gwen becomes a spiritual seeker to progress, and alternately heals and releases or is uplifted and amused by her plethora of past lives. She suffers through the terror of two Dark Nights of the Soul and over time reconnects more deeply with her Spirit Guides, Angels, ancestors, animals, and with God.

Her life is transformed when a Mystic heals her with the indescribably beautiful White Light of the Universe and gives Gwen the gift of a Reiki life-force energy attunement. She receives unconditional love, wisdom and support from many healers, family and friends.

Gwen surmounts significant pain and heartbreak during a wild roller coast ride to increase her soul energy vibration from 3D to 5D and higher. She learns we are all 'Saints and Sinners,' sense of humor is a life requirement, and John Lennon had it pitch-perfect: 'Peace and love are eternal.'

'The Flow II: Restoring the Divine Feminine'

Gwendolyn Rose begins to sense her identity and purpose as she continues to rapidly spiritually awaken. Her life purpose includes restoring the balance between the Divine Feminine and the Divine Masculine.

She continues to make past life pilgrimages to close out old energy that no longer serves her, and to master profound soul-level lessons.

The painful implications of seeing another woman wearing the same unique amber necklace as Gwen's cause her to fall apart emotionally. She unexpectedly reunites with a beloved sister from 2,000 years ago when she hands a stranger her own cherished necklace that she knows she is not meant to wear again.

Gwen begins to connect profoundly with Isis, Mary Magdalen, Mother Mary, Quan Yin and other representatives of the Divine Feminine. She receives critical assistance from a wide variety of healers on both sides of the Veil.

Gwen is stunned to realize she is one of the souls who volunteered to bring Heaven to Earth in the form of the peace, love and joy energies.

'The Flow III: Mary Magdalen Remembers'

Gwendolyn Rose continues to experience a fast-paced, profound spiritual awakening. She is stunned by the scope and implications of her own hypnotherapy sessions in the summer of 2014.

Three of Gwen's friends have their own private sessions that same week. They agree not to discuss their experiences until all four regressions are complete.

Yet all four women travel to critical points of intersection in Egypt and Jerusalem separately during their own session. Each confirms the other's presence and identity in that lifetime often referred to as 'The Greatest Mystery on Earth.'

Gwen's extensive memories as Magdalen include the Egyptian Temple of Isis, one of the Mystery Schools. She reunites with her beloved 2,000 years earlier as Mary at the well outside the temple, and they agree to marry.

But Mary is instead forced to marry John, a prophet for God, upon her return to Jerusalem. She is soon widowed by a barbarous act and given a horrific item in a basket in an attempt to control her.

Mary reunites with her beloved a second time after her first husband's death, and they joyfully marry. A decade later, her adored husband agrees to be taken by Roman soldiers. Mary and her children escape by ship to Egypt after his most remarkable 'death.'

A pregnant Mary and her son and daughter later settle in France. She raises her three children alone and begins to write her autobiography.

Three decades pass. Mary's final fear is not dying, but can she finish writing her 'Book of Love' before transitioning Home? Will her story remain safely hidden until the time returns for it to be discovered?

Made in the USA
Columbia, SC
26 May 2019